Clare

A NOVEL

JOHN MacKENNA

14.10.93

For Pauline —

Who knows there was a
life before all this
and will be after
it's over!!

[signature]

THE
BLACKSTAFF
PRESS

BELFAST

● **A BLACKSTAFF PAPERBACK ORIGINAL** ●

**Blackstaff Paperback Originals present new writing, previously
unpublished in Britain and Ireland, at an affordable price.**

First published in 1993 by
The Blackstaff Press Limited
3 Galway Park, Dundonald, Belfast BT16 0AN, Northern Ireland
with the assistance of
The Arts Council of Northern Ireland

© John MacKenna, 1993
All rights reserved

Typeset by the Northern Whig Limited, Belfast
Printed by The Guernsey Press Company Limited

A catalogue record for this book
is available from the British Library

ISBN 0-85640-467-5

for
Dolores MacKenna,
Catherine Shirley
and David Walsh

The poems quoted in *Clare* are taken from *John Clare: Selected Works,* edited by Eric Robinson and David Powell, Oxford Authors series, Oxford University Press, 1984

CONTENTS

HISTORICAL NOTE

John Clare was born in the Northamptonshire village of Helpston on 13 July 1793. He was the son of Parker Clare and Ann Stimson; his twin sister died within a fortnight. Two more girls were born into the family, of whom only one, Sophy, reached adulthood.

When Clare was at school he formed a friendship with Mary Joyce, the daughter of a local farmer. She remained his lifelong obsession, even after her death in 1838.

Having worked as a gardener, a gang labourer, a lime-burner and a harvester, Clare had his first collection of poetry, *Poems Descriptive of Rural Life and Scenery*, published in 1820 – the same year in which he married Martha 'Patty' Turner. The wedding took place on 16 March and their first daughter, Anna, was born on 1 June. Another daughter, Eliza, was born on 16 June 1822. He continued to publish poetry: *The Village Minstrel* (1821); *The Shepherd's Calendar* (1827); and *The Rural Muse* (1835). In 1832, Clare and his family moved to a cottage in Northborough, a village near Helpston.

During his lifetime Clare was befriended by a number of patrons, some more generous and undemanding than others. In this book Lady Kettering is a composite of these various individuals.

From childhood Clare had suffered what appear to have been epileptic attacks: by 1837 the severity of these fits combined with the delusions he was experiencing led to him being admitted to High Beach asylum in Essex. In July 1841 he escaped and walked the eighty miles to Northborough. He remained there until December of that year, when he was committed to St Andrew's asylum in Northampton. This was to be his home until his death on 20 May 1864.

I AM

1

I am – yet what I am, none cares or knows;
  My friends forsake me like a memory lost: –
I am the self-consumer of my woes; –
  They rise and vanish in oblivion's host,
Like shadows in love's frenzied stifled throes: –
And yet I am, and live – like vapours tost

2

Into the nothingness of scorn and noise, –
  Into the living sea of waking dreams,
Where there is neither sense of life or joys,
  But the vast shipwreck of my lifes esteems;
Even the dearest, that I love the best
Are strange – nay, rather stranger than the rest.

3

I long for scenes, where man hath never trod
  A place where woman never smiled or wept
There to abide with my Creator, God;
  And sleep as I in childhood, sweetly slept,
Untroubling, and untroubled where I lie,
The grass below – above the vaulted sky.

I

Sophy Clare

I WAS A WITNESS AT THEIR WEDDING, you know. Him and Patty. Martha was her proper name but the only time I ever heard it used was that day in the church when they exchanged their promises and I stood by as witness. I got married myself, but at a later time. I remember that day of mine but no better than his day. Me beside Patty, and her uncle John beside him. And I remember the rain and wind that day. A March wind whipping in off the fens and rattling the door of the church while we shivered at the altar.

If you asked me to say what kind of life that might make for, I'd say the day was all wrong – and the circumstances too – but it was not the way things turned out at all. It was as good a marriage as most and if there was a failing, it was his. But still. Afterwards there was little enough of celebration. Had it been the summer, we might have danced a little or had some songs, but, as I told you, it wasn't a day for dancing or the like. Not a day for doing more than getting on with it.

Now my day, my wedding day, that was a different day. The year of the Lord eighteen hundred and twenty-four. I was twenty-six years old and not unhandsome. And I'll say no more than that about myself. That day, and I walking to the church, a sheep came out across the road and made right towards me, straight as a hawk's fall, until it nuzzled my dress.

'That's for luck,' John said.

I wasn't so sure but I took his word on it. He was always a one for the lore and the stories. And he played his fiddle for my dance, and he sang one of his songs. He wrote songs, you know, and not just verses. It's the songs I remember best and love the best. I could sing twenty of them if you asked me to. He wrote the most tender songs. Such warming words and singing tunes. I was so proud of him. So proud of everything he did.

I never bury my face in a lilac flower without thinking of him. That smell, that heavy scent of being lost inside the summer, is his smell. And the willow falling to the river's edge, that is where I see him still. Sat there under the arch of the leaves with the Round Oak Waters humming. I still expect, when I pass a lilac hedge, to meet him walking in the lane, to hear him singing some rude verse and laughing to himself.

Not that it was always so. If I tell you the truth, there were days when he was the bane of my life. And I courting, he was forever getting up to his tricks and laying in wait until I'd be settled with some boy and then I'd hear him singing from the branches of a tree above our heads. Singing, you know, quiet, but not so quiet that he couldn't be heard. I never forget one summer evening and a boy kissing me in the churchyard. It was dusk and I was kissing him as much as he was kissing me and then this low voice started singing from beneath a table stone above one of the graves near where we were sat. I knew that voice and I knew those lewd words. Had our mother not forbidden John to sing them in the house?

> A maiden head, the virgins trouble,
> Is well compared to a bubble
> On a navigable river
> – Soon as touch'd 'tis gone for ever.

That boy sat there a minute, petrified, and then he fled before I had the time to tell him who it was. Not that I could have. How could I say, oh, it's only my brother lying under the stone?

And then I heard John laughing and he crept out, swung me by the arms, hugged me, and said: 'He ran and left you. Anyone who would run and leave you is not worth having.'

I told him, I said it to him, 'If I want to run him off,' I said, 'let me be the one to decide that. I don't need you deciding for me.' I told him straight to his face. I was angry with him.

But it wasn't always a tale of jesting. There was a strangeness about John. It went back – or so my mother said – to his delivery. He was a weak thing, she always said, one of a pair. The other was a bonny, ruddy sister, healthy as a parson, but there's the peculiar thing, she was dead within a two week. Faded away like light after the sun has gone. Our other sister, Elizabeth, she died too. But John struggled on. And even when he was as hardy as the other children, he was still the pet lamb in our house.

My mother could neither read nor write herself but her hopes and plans were always high for John. One time he could be a schoolmaster, the next a clerk, and the next again something grander. Oh, how she fussed over that boy, fussed and cockered him. I'd see her in church, singing out above the rest, singing 'Lo, He comes with clouds descending', her voice shaking in the rafters, and suddenly she'd leave off in the middle of the

'hallelujah' and turn to John and see if he was warm
enough or well enough. Or close enough. She was
always keeping him close to her. In church or at home
or in the fields. Not that he was one for hanging about
her but she seemed to need reminding every so often
that he was alive and well and wasn't going to slip away
like his twin sister.

And there's another thing. I'd overhear her talk of
learning as 'the blackest art' and yet she had us set on
learning, him and me, trotting us off to Master Seaton's
school in Glinton church.

You know, I think sometimes my fear of the night
and the dead came of playing among the gravestones at
our recreation time. John was forever jumping at me
from behind the stones. He seemed to find great ease
among the dead. Him and Richard Turnill and Mary
Joyce would sit among the farthest stones as though they
were at home. The rest of us would stay as close to the
vestry door as our games would allow. But not that
three.

My mother said that he had come as near to death in
childhood as he could and it held no fear for him. 'More
of it,' I'd say, 'more of the pet lamb.' I'd say it to his face.
I'd run along the lane and shout at him like a sheep.
'You're the pet lamb,' I'd say. 'Baa,' I'd say. If he was
with his friends, with the Turnill boys or Mary Joyce,
he'd be most annoyed and that would please me all the

more. 'The pet lamb, John Clare,' I'd shout. 'Baa, our John, and baa again.'

Oh, he would be enraged, you know, and threaten all kinds of torture on me, but I would laugh. I knew him well enough not to fear what he said. Not that he was always the lamb himself. Sometimes, even he would be overcome by the weight of my mother's concern and he would ask her to let him be. And sometimes he would slip her lead in church and sit with the boys at the back and sing bawdy words to the hymns. 'Away with our sorrow and our care' was one they had a liking for. And when I say a liking, it was not for singing that as Wesley intended.

I think my mother caught him between the weakly child he was and the man our father wanted him to be. I think her expectations and our father's expectations were like two crosses laid across John's shoulders.

'An open hand is no lure for a hawk,' my mother would say. 'You must hope to rise if rise you will.'

'Rise?' our father would laugh. 'The lad can hardly rise from bed without your lending him a hand.'

And then they'd be off about his future and his worth and his prospects. Not that our father stopped John or me, you know. He never stopped us out of school beyond the times when we were needed in the fields. At harvest and the like. He saw some sense in schooling but he never had the hopes our mother had.

'That,' she would say, when he was not about, 'is because of his past. He likes nothing better than to set people together by the ears.'

What she meant was that our father was a bastard, though I never heard her say as much. She believed all his sourness stemmed from that. Not that he was continually sour. I would not be the one to say that. His sourness grew with his age and so did his illness, and I think the two grew of one root and my mother, being ill herself and not complaining, could not see that fact. But there, I have gone off down a lane of my own making and left you no nearer the place you were going.

John. He was not like our father or our mother. Neither one in particular. And not like me. He had some of my wildness, or I had some of his, but he was darker than me. I think he carried some of his sister's passing with him through his life. When things were good for him, he missed something of her, and when he missed her, he seemed to find a passion to make up for her loss. He was close to me, you know, but always there was a shadow walking between us. The shadow of our sister or of Richard Turnill or of Mary Joyce, and it made my flesh creep. I tell you, this is truth.

Still, that was only part of it. There were other, better, parts. Let me tell you those. How he'd swing me in his arms, up into the apple tree. Our apple tree. That tree. I must explain to you.

We lived in a cottage that had four apartments and in each apartment was a family. The garden was divided too, and in our division was an apple tree. In winter it would sparkle like a gewgaw and we would watch it in the winter sun, the branches flashing like swimmers in standing water. And in spring the flowers weighed it almost to the grass and then the flowers fell and the leaves were lifted for a while before the apples, small as stones at first, began to lower themselves and grow. That tree paid our rent for years. And it gave us children a place to play. John would swing me high into that tree and I would close my eyes and jump out into the air and always know that he would catch me in his arms. He wasn't strong but he was strong enough. Oh, such games! Just him and me. Just John and me and I screaming in the garden, my dress flying like a wash in the air and John's sure arms catching me and holding me and my feet touching the grass as soft as a leaf. I was a leaf that fell and fell and never once got trodden on.

That tree was everything then. To climb in, to swing in, to pick fruit from. Every morning in the autumn time we would collect the windfalls from the grass and my mother would walk round and round the tree and point to the apples that were ready for picking. And John and me would scramble through the branches, following her orders.

He would make a game of it, naming the apples for

the planets and the stars. 'We cannot take that one, Mother, for that would leave us without sun.' Or moon or some other planet of his liking and my mother would laugh and tell him to pass on and then, and we walking to school, he would produce the sun-apple for Mary Joyce, without a word.

And other times John and me would watch our father digging in the garden. His great back bent and the huge clods that he lifted like dead grass. Tossed above his head and caught and shook on their way down. He would worry the clay from a clod and leave it lifeless at the side of a drill. Then he'd call to us to come and gather up the grasses and burn them. And sometimes he would throw the fork to John and say: 'You turn a sod, lad, time is coming for you to do it.'

John would struggle, you know, struggle to lift the heavy clay and our father would take the fork and fling a clod up into the morning sky and catch it and shake it and laugh at John.

'Weak as water,' he'd say. 'And your mother is steady as time.'

'And what am I?' I'd ask.

'You, Sophy, are lovely as a lily,' our father would say.

For the most part, days were good then. I never remember any great trouble and certainly none that could compare with what come afterwards. Days of work or days of schooling. Nights at the fire or in visiting, or nights in dancing as the season set. And John at his fiddling in our house or another house or, sometimes, at James Merrishaw's night school. Even when he was a boy, I recall him fiddling and reading and making up his verses and songs. Whatever troubles there were, they were little as dust. Nothing like what they became. Nothing

For fun, our mother would ask John, and he nine or ten, to recite by heart from the Bible, and he would always say from Job. He had a fondness for Job. There was one verse, I recall, that frightened me: 'And the Lord said unto Satan, Whence comest thou? Then Satan answered the Lord, and said, From going to and fro in the earth, and from walking up and down in it.'

I would think of that and I walking to and fro myself and when I used to be sitting in the churchyard during school and I'd expect to meet the devil face to face. I daren't tell that to John. He would have reminded me of it in the nighttime or on evenings when I was setting out to walk alone. He was forever doing that but sometimes I thought it was odd, this peace he had among the dead and yet how he was fearful of the demons that lurked in sunless, haunted places.

All these things. I keep returning to these things without meaning to. I can only make sense of it as that shadow that forever fell between us. Always cast by someone or other and not always the same source but always that same coldness. Not that I didn't love him. I loved him with the thickness of blood and the closeness of sister. But a shadow has a way of coming between things.

I could tell you a hundred things we did in our childhood. We climbed, we sang, we stole birds' eggs, we swam, we hunted snails, we worked with our father, we sat in the same school room, we laughed, we talked and we slept in the same bed and I cannot say in which circumstances that shadowy mist fell. It was not in everyone but it came, and finally it stayed, though by then it was a heavier and more sorrowful affair. But I will not try to explain it away as just my nature. It was more than that. Much more.

John was always following some road: mathematics; poems; fiddling; songs; the thought of schoolmastering; scribbling on sugar bags. But I never believed he would reach a destination. I was proud of him but that darkness fell between us and then fell thicker and thicker on him. And when the crosses our mother and father laid on him were gone at last, he had found his own slow sadness. As though he needed it, as though he could not make his way without a pain inside himself, as though he felt less full without this suffering. Does that make any sense at all?

I'm not always given to this kind of thinking but when I look back, you know, at times like this, these are the things that come to mind and come without my being able to stop them or without my asking them. Good things and darker things, and often the darker things hang like a gauze across the brighter. Or hang there just at the edge. Like as if they were waiting. Now I know that sounds odd, or worse, but every time I look back or think back that strangeness, that blackness, is there between us or around us.

I remember, and I a girl out courting, I would dread the sight of a crowd along the roadway. Any crowd anywhere scared me because I never knew until I came upon it whether our John would be in the midst of it. It might not matter now – although I cannot say, not for certain – but then, and I a girl of sixteen and seventeen, it put a fright on me. I'd be walking with some lad and we'd see people huddled on the road and I'd think at once that John must be lying there among them in one of his terrible attacks. He would be taken by these attacks and fall down speechless but not soundless. He would scream and cry and kick and claw until he lost the energy to continue.

Our father said these fits went back to a day at harvesting. He told me John was team-leading the horses for the Turnills and one of the loaders, I think Thomas Drake, fell from the top of a wagon and was killed. His neck was broke and John saw it all. He was standing at the horses' head and Drake fell forward. Our father said everyone in the team heard the crack of his neck when it broke and John heard it most of all, he being the nearest. He went into a weakness straight away with fright, and then these fits and turns began. He told me once, lying in his bed at home, that he always knew when he was about to fall because a coldness would start in his feet and move through his body and he would lose all feeling. But whatever the cause, it would always occupy my fears when I saw a crowd in the lane. Sometimes, and I don't mind confessing this, I would walk on and hope that no one would call out to me that my brother was taken so. I would count to twenty and five, the sum of the figures in my birth year and always my number, and think if none had called me by then that it were not our John that had drawn the crowd together.

But oftentimes the call came. 'Sophy Clare,' they'd call, 'your brother is taken mad again.'

I might try to walk on, hoping his friends would come to his assistance, but more oftentimes than not I was left to tend him and bring him back home when he came to himself. Always, after his madnesses, he would be weak as water. Even in winter days he would sweat and sweat and we would have to dawdle on the roadway and stop every twenty yards or thereabouts.

I saw him once one January after he had taken a turn and fallen into a whitethorn hedge. His face and neck were cut and I had the skin torn from my hands in trying to help him out and he a leaden weight. In the end Morgan the carpenter came by and lifted him clear and laid him on the grass. It was hoary and hard but he lay there a long time without stirring. So long I thought he was dead. So long that when I got him to his feet the shape of his body was left on the frost – the very shape of his body through the frost.

At other times when we were walking from school, John and the Turnills and Mary Joyce and me, he would stop and sit by the road and try to let the madness pass by, staying very still, but that never worked. He would go into a weakness and we would wait until he came out of it again, and then walk on, carrying him between us. But one thing I must say, and I have always said this, I never heard the Turnills or Mary Joyce laugh or call after him as the others did, about his madness, you know. Never.

My mother's greatest fear was that he should be taken with a turn somewhere out on the fens and fall into the water and be drowned. One day in spring, and John fifteen or so, Richard Turnill told me he was walking a lane and saw a flock of crows grazing close to the woods and a dark patch in their midst, out near Wormstalls' farm this was, and he was about to pass on when something turned his path. He might as easily have walked on, he told me, might not even have seen the form had he been looking the other way, but when the

crows scattered into the trees he saw clearly that it was
our John sprawled senseless in the grass. He might have
lain there all day and night had Richard not come upon
him. That time he was without speech for all of the day
and night and some of the next day too. Lying up on his
bed with his eyes open but not speaking. I brought him
up a cup of broth and his eyes were staring at the roof
and there was not a movement in them. This time, I
thought, he is dead and I turned to go back down and
tell my mother, but he sighed and I knew he was still
there.

That was his worst time of all, knowing none of us.
The doctor came and looked at him and muttered and
sighed, but could do nothing until John found the way
back for himself. My mother told me not to ask him
about what had happened, not to talk of it to him.

The Turnills came and sat with him that day and the
next and Richard said he believed John would mend or
die. He said that to me in the garden out our front. 'If
he gets worse he will die,' he said. 'But I think the worst
is over.'

That was Richard's way, to face the worst and then
to find a better hope. I loved him dearly. Of all John's
friends he was the truest and kindest. Once, one
Christmas time, and we dancing in his house, he took
my hand and held it for an hour or more and kissed me,
and we leaving and he told me he thought of me all the

time. That was the Christmas before he fell ill himself. If he was about, and John in his madnesses, I would never fear. He would stay with John and talk to him and take him home.

But so often there was only me, you know, and all I could do was tell whoever had gathered to stand back and leave him be, that he would come better himself, if only they would leave him be. It got to a time when people knew this and once he had finished his yelling and kicking they left him to me and went their way.

I would sit by him and chatter. Not for his sake but for my own. To keep myself from thinking of what was happening and the things that might yet happen. I would remind him of the games we played as children. Snail-hunting in the fields. That was a favourite of ours.

But it wasn't always so. These mists grow with remembering. There were other times and other days that were happier, brighter. Times when the mists were distant from us or fell so weakly that we didn't see them or feel their icy breath on our necks. Days in the sun when we brought our father's dinner up to him in the fields. Me carrying the bread and cheese, John swinging a can of beer round and round and the beer staying inside, even when it was upside down.

'If it spills our father will kill you,' I'd say.

'It cannot spill,' John would say, shaking his head. 'It cannot spill out if I twirl it fast enough.'

And sure enough, it never did.

Sometimes John would race across the grass and hide among the elms and I would shout at him to wait and he would spring out to frighten me and laugh at my fear. Other days, and we all at school, we would leapfrog home together. Five of us in a line down the long lane. The Turnills and John and Mary Joyce and me. Leapfrogging all that way. Five children laughing so that our voices sent a new warmth through the hedges and the fens. And hopscotching. John made us a rhyme for hopscotch. A rhyme of our own, known only to the five of us. The first rhyme of his that I recall. 'And one is sticks and two is stones and three is hope and four is bones and five is living and six is dying and seven is walking and eight is flying.' That was how it went.

'Say it soft if there's anyone about,' John would tell me. 'This is ours and we must keep it.'

And we did. I never heard another soul say that rhyme.

'Always dying and bones and the like,' Mary Joyce said, when John spoke the rhyme over to us. 'You always talk of that.'

Curious that she should have been the one to mention it. But all that was to come much later. And John was always going on at me, you know, with stories of weird happenings. Not that he was alone in that. My mother was forever telling strange stories and the lower the wick grew the more frightening the stories grew. Stories about witches and goblins and fairies. Fairies that slipped through the keyholes at night and stole children away. Bold children. I thought then that they had stolen our sisters away from us. I said it once to my mother and she stopped that story ever afterwards.

When we were abed, I'd lie and listen to the mice scratching in the eaves and hear John's steady breathing beside me and imagine all the witches flying by in the blackness outside. From Deeping Gate to Southorpe, from Newborough to Bainton, and all of them swishing over Helpston and scraping the twigs of their brooms on the window of our room. John asleep and me saying over and over the prayers we had said together at our bedside: 'Bless us, Lord, and bless our home. Bless our father, bless our mother. Keep us pure and watch and guard us through the night.' And still the witches flicked our window and still he slept and still I could not find a place to sleep.

But then the summer would come and I'd think no more of witches or fairies or dying in the darkness. I'd think only of games to play and freedom to run and sun to light the evenings and our father singing in the fields. There was one song he sang that my mother chastised him for (she would never hear it sung within the house), but our father sang it anyway, outside in the garden or in the fields or on the lane and he walking.

As I and Molly Baily went along the greenwood side,
with some soft words we did concert that she should
be my bride.
My instrument was well in tune and she in tune would keep
and frankly we did then presume to find a happy sleep.
My instrument was well in tune and she in tune would keep
and frankly we did then presume to find a happy sleep.

If our father was intent on making my mother rage he
would sing that song softly in her hearing but change the
name to Annie Stimson, my mother's name before
marrying. And she would tell him to hold his mouth and
he would walk outside and go on singing in the garden,
louder and louder as the song went on.

Each part did well in concert move, the whisper I did heed
And oh such melting strains of love that she cried out
with me.
Our music was such charming sweet, we played it
three times o'er
but when I could no more repeat she laughed and
cried encore.

There, I remember it as well as when I knew it first.
I sang it once to my own husband and he scolded me.

'No woman should be heard singing that kind of
song,' he said.

'My father sang it,' I said back, as sharp as a needle.

He nodded and coughed and said he was not surprised,
knowing that would anger me. For I had made the
mistake of telling my husband that my father was a

bastard and ever since he has taken it upon himself to treat my father's memory as though every failing was to be expected and every virtue was an accident. If someone, in conversation, refers to my father's singing or his drinking or his wrestling, my husband will cough his little cough, the same cough he gives in church when he is passing out the plate for collection, and smile a smile that is neither warm nor sweet. Some day I will find a word about his churchgoing and put it in where it will halt his gallop. Not yet, but some day.

Richard Turnill would not have been like that. He would have remembered the better things about our father. His music and his great laugh that was like thunder. And his storytelling. Our father could hold us silent for an hour, silent on our form in the winter, silent under the apple tree in the summer. Silent as a fly in the web of his stories. Or walking home on harvest nights, down the lanes, he would start up a story, sometimes that same story that has come back to darken my own dark days. The story about Jane the barmaid in Barholm.

Jane was always searching for a lover, for a man who would love her the whole life through. Anyone who wanted her would come to the inn where she worked and when she got some notion that this might be the one she would take them up to her room and lie with them. Sometimes two in a night, our father said, and always in the hope that this might be the one who would stay. But they all left her afore morning, he said, took her and left. Men came from as far distant as Upton and Glinton to lie with her and leave her. He had met with men himself, our father said, and he a young boy walking to work in the summer mornings, and he would stop to talk with them in the road and they would tell him how they were returning from a night with Jane.

But there was one young farmer who frequented the inn and Jane fell in love with him and he with her, or so it seemed, and she stopped lying with the other men and lay only with him. They walked out together and she lived for him. Then he got her with child and when she told him, he denied her, denied her there in the inn, before all the other men.

The next night she was found hanging in her room, with her face to the window, our father said, and her eyes burning like the deepest coals in hell. They couldn't be closed, he said. And where to bury her? Church gates were closed to her and none would hear of her being buried in or near Barholm. So the landlord of the inn had her body taken by night and buried on the waste patch at the crossroads in Helpston, where the Upton and Barnack roads meet. The same crossroads me and John would pass in going for the milk.

It was a story told in the light and with our father beside us but a story that came back to haunt us on darksome evenings when the wind spoke through the throat of that barmaid and the few leaves and battered trees managed to twist themselves into the shape of a woman and her unborn infant.

Our father's stories and his way in telling them were that good that they went on long after they had been told. My husband could snap all he liked but there was no story he could tell that had the power of our father's tales.

But there were other things too, you know, that I would never tell my husband for fear of him casting them up to me. I loved my father very much and I loved the way that his laughter could make a summer evening seem brighter than it was. I never feared for us when he had his strength. Watching him dig our garden or fell a tree or carry its trunk home on his shoulders and split it for our fire gave me courage. But there was a chillier side – not that I believe that he meant to cause John pain. He was intent only on trying to make him sturdy, to give him the toughness to get on with his life and to come out of the sickness and weakness that cursed him.

Our father would take John into the garden on summer evenings and show him how to hold and wrestle. And each lesson would end in a match between our father and John. They would face up to each other in the grass and my mother would come and stand at the gable's end and sometimes people passing in the road would stop to watch. Round and round they'd go, eyeing each other, rushing, backing, testing, and then suddenly our father would have John in his grip and then flat upon his back, his shoulders hard against the clay. Then he'd back away, you know, to let John up and they would face to each other once again. Sometimes our father would fall and John would leap on him but in a twist our father would be out from under him like a fish and John would be pinned again. Our father would give a great hearty laugh and pull him to his feet and square to him again. It might go on for an hour like that until our father grew weary of always winning and shouted at John and told him to fight like a man.

'Last fight,' our father would shout. 'Last fight, put all your strength in this.' And he would run at John and have him on his back in a blink.

'Mind that boy's head,' my mother would shout and my father would swear quietly and turn John with one last throw and leave him face down in the warm grass.

'You'll never be a fighter, boy,' he'd say, 'unless you learn to fight.'

Then he'd walk away. Often as not John would be up and after him, launching himself onto our father's back like a hawk on a mouse, and laughing. But not always. There were times, after our father had gone into the house, when I heard John sobbing with pain and frustration and anger. He never cried aloud and our father never knew he cried, but I did. I never told our father for he would have said something to John and that would have been worse. But he should have known when to stop. Or so I've always thought. But I would never mention that to my husband, you know, for he would store it and use it when he thought it most hurtful to me. That is the pass we've come to in our lives.

There I go again, shadows again. I mustn't let you think it was all, or even mostly, like that. We threshed with him, my mother and us and our father. Working in the fields together. And all of us seated in farmers' kitchens eating together and my mother laughing because she did not have to cook the food and could enjoy it all the more.

Best of all was the threshing up at Turnills'. I would get to work side by side with Richard and the work never seemed as hard for that. Much more of laughing and playing than at any other farm. I know now that was because of my fondness for Richard and his company but then, and I a girl, it seemed the Turnill harvest was always easier and quicker and the food laid out was always better and we worked more as a team together. Our father and mother in the field, John at the horses' head and me racing about at all kinds of doings and all the while trying to keep Richard in my eyes. There! Not one shadow or finger of coldness in that.

But there were times, too, when our father would show great kindness to John. I recall a time when John went on and on at our father about a book he wanted, a book of verse, for one shilling and six pennies, and in the end our father gave him the money and John walked to Stamford to buy his book but the shop was closed, it being a Sunday. And the following Tuesday he walked there again and came back home carrying his possession proudly. Or so I recollect it, though once, and John and me talking about it, he said it was not so. He told me I remembered it wrong. He told me he sneaked back through the village, climbing into the fields and waiting until dusk, for fear of being seen and called a crazy boy.

They did call him a crazy boy when he went walking with a book in his hand. Not all of them, not the Turnills or Mary Joyce, but there were many that did. Richard Turnill was a true friend to John. And to me. But in a particular way to John.

I may be mistaken on that recollection of John walking home with the book. It may be that he remembered it more correctly but I have my own memory of an evening in January — and this I can swear upon the Bible — and I out the lane. It was dusk. A muslin of snow was hanging on the pastures and there was more in the sky, blowing in from Peakirk and Newborough. I was making for home and the snow behind me and for some reason I cannot recall, or there may have been no reason at all, I turned to search the road behind me for company and there, coming out of the falling darkness and confusion of snow, were three figures walking carelessly in my footsteps. Our John and Mary Joyce and Richard Turnill. Two of them with coats pulled up about their faces, all but Mary Joyce, whose shawl was wrapped about her, leaving her hair free in the chill wind. I stopped in the shelter of a bush and waited for them to come on. They had not noticed me. The three of them linked arm in arm and laughing, as I heard when they came near enough for me to hear above the whistle of the wind and the damping of the snow. Their faces were white with snow and their hands would sweep, from time to time, wiping the frozen blizzard from their skins.

How strange to think of that occasion. There must be a thousand others when John walked with them or with others, or when I myself walked with Richard and Mary, and yet that is the picture I return to, in waking and in sleep, time and time. Three pale figures on the snowy road from Glinton. I can only think that they had gone to call on Mary Joyce and she was coming with them to the Turnills' when the snow came after them, and they carried on their laughing way without a thought for it. She cannot have been coming to our cottage for I have no remembrance of any time in all our lives when she stood on our kitchen floor, not even as a child. But this time that I recall was when Richard was seventeen or so. None of us was still a child.

There is another night I call to mind, when Richard and John and me were walking late. We had gone out into the fen to watch the stars and we were returning home. It was a late night and there was a full moon imprinted on the sky. We came down by the church. It had just been slated at that time and the moon was skating down its grey back. We stopped to look at this and John sighed and said: 'There is no other good in that place than the sight of the moon on its roof.'

He was always against the church and clergy. Always railing and ranting at home about them and then disappearing of a Sunday, out across the fens or deep into the woods, when it was church time. Yet he knew his hymns and said his prayers but he would not go inside the church. It drowned his light, he said, as no river could.

Our father would bang the table of a Saturday night and tell John he must go.

'And listen to them bend the word of God to fit their fences and their rights?' John would say.

'You will be there,' our father would say, very quietly but very sternly, after he had finished slapping his fist upon the wood. 'You will be there.'

But there was never an hour early enough for our father to catch John before he was gone into the woods. In summertime I fancy he stole out in the night and slept in the fields. He was always a great one for sleeping out was John. I think our father went through this ritual to satisfy himself that he had done his duty by the Lord and John went through his to satisfy his own stubbornness. Perhaps it was our father he was besting and not the clergymen at all. Or both.

But still. Let me tell you something that may make you think me crazy too. Some nights, in the pitchy days of the turning of the year, when I am sitting at my fireside and my husband is well asleep and the wind is blowing in hard against the windowpane, carrying a bonnet of snow, I pull back the curtain and press my face against the glass, feeling the draught upon my cheek, and slowly come to recognise the furniture of our yard in the white covering. The pump, the hedges, the fencing, the gateposts, and beyond them the roadway. And I wait there, fancying I see the three figures walking from the storm. Even in the blackness I see Mary Joyce's shawl, red about her shoulders, growing paler by the moment, until she shakes it, and suddenly it is red again. John with his head thrown sidewards, laughing. His drab, thin coat wrapped about him like a sheet, taking his shape in its wetness. And Richard Turnill, whose clothing I can never recall, his bright eyes in the dull day as they came close to where I was standing, sheltered.

It was he who saw me first and he did not say a word to them but walked straight towards me and smiled and said my name. 'Sophy.'

That was enough. I think it is he I miss the most of all. His voice. His face.

I know the life I had as far as John was concerned. It was as good or as bad as it was meant to be. It was beyond my power to change. And as for Mary Joyce, we all of us should have seen what would happen there. That was beyond all our powers to change. We might as well have tried to keep the pastures unfenced for the hope we should have had.

But for Richard, there might have been something as far as my existence was concerned. I feel there was, you know. And when the others walk on past our gate, on nights like that, I wish them well but I fancy Richard comes and stands in recognition of what might have been between us. I think my fancy in this matter is a great degree less than John's was in his expectations of Mary Joyce. But then, perhaps, we are all inclined to see what we would. We forgive those who forgive us. We do unto others as we would have them do to us. Or so my husband prays at church.

I will speak no more about my imaginings for Richard but I must relate the last time he and I were together. It was Eastertide and we went walking in search of John and found him seated, fishing, beneath a willow. The tree was flaming with catkins and John was soon telling us about goat willows and grey willows and eared willows and I was anxious that Richard and I might go on walking together. But we did not. Instead we sat with John, and thereafter I always thought of willows as a curse, you know, but not in a great way. Not like sickness or death or ruin but as a cause of frustration to me.

That is one tale I did relate to my husband and he said nothing, but an hour later he came back to me and said: 'We never called them willows. They were sallows in my parish.'

It was one of the last surprises in our life. Since then I have not been surprised by anything he might say or any road he might take from something I have said. But still, enough of him and this.

Richard Turnill died when he was nineteen years. Of the typhus. He was buried of a May morning and it was the only time I saw John go near the church without complaining, and the least happy time of all.

The whitethorn was hanging out across the path through the churchyard, brushing our faces as we followed after his coffin. John told me afterwards he heard it brush against the side of the coffin. Weeks afterwards. One day in June when we were sitting in our garden. I was sewing and John was noting his plants in a book. He would take each flower and hold it up against the sky and say its name and then write that in his book. I recall some of those names even yet: Solomon's seal; a late-flowering yellow star-of-Bethlehem;

the columbine; monkshood; and the creeping buttercup. These I remember, perhaps not from that day but from another. Or perhaps I remember them from that day too.

When all his plants were listed and put into his book he closed it and said very quietly to me: 'I heard the whitethorn scrape against the side of Richard's coffin.'

I said nothing because I might have heard it too, but I had no memory of anything beyond my own sorrow from that day. No recollection of any sense but dread.

'I heard the whitethorn scrape along the side of the coffinwood,' he said, 'and I thought it was his fingers scratching to be free, to walk out across the fens with me. To walk into the night and watch the great plough that ploughs the skies. I all but called out to his father to lift the coffin lid.'

And still I was silent. Half frightened at the thought that Richard might have gone to his grave still breathing, though I knew the typhus had swept him from our lives. But I was frightened, too, at the thought of what my brother's screaming in the churchyard might have done to those of us about. Madness mixed with grief is a terrifying thought.

I was at a loss for words but then I said: 'Tell me the other plants you have in your book, John.'

And he did. Carefully he turned his pages and I pretended an interest in the pale flowers pressed flat upon the paper. Cowslips and false oxlips, whose delicate yellow had yellowed the pages into which they had been pressed. The tall and ghostly poet's narcissus, a flower born for my brother if ever one was born for one man. Salsify with its twisted leaves. Spotted medick and black medick with their three-cornered leaves. The bold forget-me-not, cold there in its page, a reminder of the words my brother had just spoken.

'What next?' I urged, turning the page for him. 'What else is there that you have not shown me? Show me more.'

I wanted him to go on turning his pages, I wanted those dead flowers to continue in procession and stop out all need for words and all thought of the dead boy, the only one who might have helped us both. The only one to hold John and listen to his gibbering and keep him close when the shaking came and his senses were gone. The only one to take him home and see him into his bed and sit with him until his mind returned. The only one to shake him out of his terrible despair. The only one whose face made mine a mirror of delight.

I cannot say that Richard Turnill's death cast that shadow between John and me. It might have been cast by the other dead children or by our own lives and the people that we were but I do believe his light might have kept the desolation at bay. When his light went out the shadow seemed to settle more firmly on our hopes.

But a thing more frightening still was to come of that. One evening in the harvest time, and we walking home together, John went back to our talk of Richard's burial.

'Do you recall the day of Richard's burying?' he asked me.

As if it was something I could forget, as if it was something a hundred years before. 'I remember,' I said.

'By God but it was hot. And all that mass of people and yet the quietness. So quiet I heard the whitethorn scrape against his coffin. I thought for a long time afterwards he was scraping the wood.'

'I know that, John,' I said.

'It was the whitethorn,' he said, very slowly and very simply and I was terrified by that slowness, that way in which he spoke. Terrified because I knew he had been wrestling with this for all of the summer and had only now, perhaps even this day, come to an answer in his own mind. I think I realised then, there, how bleak his future was.

I tried, at once, to take his mind off that talk (and my own, too). I made myself to smile and spoke lightly: 'Do you remember a game we played as children, John, rolling stones in our yard? Do you remember that?'

He said nothing, not one word, and we walked home in silence.

One evening, not long after that time, John was about

something in the garden and our father came out and watched and then shouted across the grass.

'You haven't wrestled me in a long time, John,' he said.

John went on with whatever he was doing.

'I fancy a turn,' our father said. He threw his coat into the branches of the apple tree and squared to John. 'Come on, lad, there's many would put a shilling down to face me yet.'

John left down whatever was in his hand and put his own coat on the grass and faced our father and they eyed each other. Our father slapped his hands against his legs a time or two and moved to one side and then the other. All the while John went on circling him and then, as quick as sticks, he had our father on the ground, his knees pressed into our father's arms, his hands upon his chest. I saw our father draw a deep breath and I waited for him to push John back. I saw his muscles strain and his face begin to purple, but there was nothing he could do. John had him pinned and he was pinned for good.

Our father lay there, with John astride him, for a good long time and then John stood and stepped back. I waited for him to offer his hand, to pull our father from the ground, but instead he walked away and picked his coat from the grass and walked out of the garden.

I went inside the house and I knew, as I should have known but had not taken notice of, that our father was broken with work. He was good for nothing but to fill in the stones on the turnpike.

All that winter he sat beside the fire and watched John writing at the table. Once I heard him say as how the table had been used for nothing but to eat from before John started at his poems and I told this to him.

'He laughs at me,' John said. 'He laughs and asks how I could ever hope to be a poet.'

'He's proud of you,' I said. 'We all are.'

John said nothing at all to that.

It seemed to me then that whatever life they should have together, under that roof, must either be brief or bitter but it was not so. They never wrestled again and there was no reply to our father whenever he commented upon John's verse-making.

And I was proud of him, proud to have him there on my wedding day, to hear him sing and play his fiddle. The vicar that married us had said somewhere that John had took his poems from other books and tried to pass them off as his own. But it was not till some months later that the word got back to John concerning this. By that time I was safely married. I shudder to think what might have fallen out on that day if he had known.

As it was, I was pleased and proud to say to my husband's people: 'This is my brother, John Clare, as has had poems published, as has been to London and knows writers and other famous people.'

That was something my husband's family could not contest. His father nodded and said, 'Soft words butter no parsnips', and went about his dull and sullen way but he could not counter John with anything of like nature on his own side.

Not that I wish you to think it was a day full of bitterness, you know. Not at all. No one, not even a queen, would have been fit partner for my husband in his family's eyes. It was not especially me that was wanting, it was but the whole world as had failed them.

I ignored that part of the day and sang, though I was careful in the choosing of what I sang. I called on John to sing and he was not so careful, and I smiled at that, and had him fiddle for our dancing. I danced with him myself and minded him of how our mother was forever finding his verses in our room and using them to scour her pots. At the year's end, what should have been enough to make a book was but a handful left on the window ledge. I gave him my clothes chest after that, the one with the lock, and our mother never knew. I took that chest with me on marrying and John left some verses in it and I have kept them still.

Oh, we laughed and danced and sang that day as we had rarely done before and have never since and never will again. I like to keep that day close to my heart. It was a day of failure in my life. I had hoped to dance my wedding dance with someone else. I had long imagined

Sophy Turnill to be the fairest name I could have dreamed of but in spite of all I made it a day of enjoyment, if not of happiness.

The fiddlers played 'Moss Roses' and I danced with John and smiled at all about me. And for that reason I like to keep its certain warmth where I can draw upon it. I remember his laughter and we dancing, his legs high flying as we brushed the walls about the room, and my husband's people uncertain as to whether he was mad or drunk or both. And my mother crying in the corner, as though she had suffered a loss of life. He minded me how she had cried, too, when he left us for a soldier. Swearing she would never see him again. And all the neighbours waving him away.

'Three hundred men from the county,' he told me afterwards, 'and I one of the shortest.'

And he told me how he hated the other men more than he could ever hope to hate the French, no matter what their crime. And in the end he struck his corporal and came marching home, disgraced but free. Our father were proud of that, of John striking a corporal. He might have done the same himself. He smiled to hear John tell of that and got him to tell the story over and over and loved it every time. I knew he felt his wrestling had been worth while. But John would never nod to that. He told the story and allowed our father some satisfaction but never the satisfaction of knowing he had trained his son that well.

I never spoke of that to John, as I never spoke of many things, and still I do not speak of much that concerns me to those I should confide in but that, you know, is not the same as not caring and not feeling. Perhaps I should not have been able to talk plainly to Richard if he had lived and I had remained his friend or something closer, but I feel we would have had an openness because he was without pretence. My husband does not believe in parading his inner thoughts and therefore does not welcome others doing it to him.

John was open in certain things but the distance he kept between our father and himself – rightly or wrongly – contributed a degree or two to the darkness of that shadow between us. So many things increased its weight. So many factors contrived to bring us where we are. And so few of late have made any light in the darkness.

Those verses I kept I never read any more, not because I do not think them good but because they are all written in a time when we were much younger and there was still a hope that things would improve. Now I see no place where improvement might come, in his life or mine.

The last thing I read from John was this letter which arrived unexpected from Northampton asylum at the start of the springtime. I had reckoned, as I opened it, a letter like the others that had come at intervals, where

John had signed himself in the name of Lord Byron. Letters full of fancy and rantings. Not letters at all, really, more the demented ramblings of a man who had forgotten who he was. But when I read this letter I felt grateful for the respite that had been his in writing it and was mine in reading it. Then, I understand, he returned to his state of removal from reality but I try not to think of that but rather of the day when he wrote this letter to me.

It was a day in April. And occasionally, when I take the letter from the box where I have stored it, I close my eyes and recall another day in April, a stormy day full of sunshine and great gusts of wind, and we walking from Northborough. We came through Etton and a mile from home John climbed into a tree, a young tree that swayed ever from east to west in the tongue of the storm. He climbed up into the highest, softest branches and swayed with it. His face towards Peakirk and into the storm coming off the fens. I stood on the road and shouted up to him to have a care but he just shouted back that I should climb into the tree and stand with him.

'I cannot,' I said. 'The storm is too strong, it is too dangerous to stand up there. I will not take the chance.'

'Then you'll never know what it feels like here,' he said and he turned his face into the wind and the look in his eyes, the smile on his mouth! He was like a child with his face buried in the strength of his mother's bosom. He had no fear of anything, he was living for that roar of the surging wind and the sun that was blown across his hair, and the uncertainty of the waving, buoyant branch that was all that kept him from the hardness of the ground thirty feet below.

I could never have stood in that tree in circumstances such as that. John could not resist the possibility. I would never fall to the ground because I would never leave it. He was certain to fall, and each time he climbed, he climbed higher so that the fall, when it came, was one from which there will never be a recovery.

But I was not always anchored to the earth. I can only hope that you see some sign in what I say, I can only hope that you guess at the things I wish to say but cannot.

But there, I was talking about the letter that came last springtime. In that letter there was hope, there was the same smile that I saw in his face that day when he climbed into the tree and embraced the storm from the east. And when I read that letter I imagine John's face as it was all those years ago, alive and eager and alert. 'Little sister,' he wrote (that was his endearment for me):

> I write this with an easy heart. I am seated in the
> open yard and the sun is upon me. I am thinking
> of a place I was used to walk with Richard

Turnill a place where we twisted sallies until
they grew into a knot. I am thinking of this
because I still have in my writing drawer a rule
that Morgan the carpenter made for me from
that tree when he felled it a good many years
after. I should have been a carpenter that would
have been a trade to put my hand to. What was
I – mason painter gardener. Do you recall they
would have made a clerk of me, our mother and
father. Do you recall from this distance as how
they sent me to Peterborough, that long journey
that I was not prepared for in a coat that was too
small and gloves that was too big and I had
nothing to say for myself and did not want to be
there in the first. I would not have made a clerk
not locked in some dull office where the sun had
not the courage to send even the weakest of its
light. I was only happy out there on the fens. I
could watch the skylarks there I would stand
with my head thrown back and my eyes fixed
directly above me and must have looked a poor
thing in that manner and you would ask me
what I was looking for and I would say skylark
the word gurgling in my throat for I would not
look away for fear of losing sight of the bird that
was a pebble out in the great celestial sea. Do
you recall me always as a child wishing to walk

to the end of the world out there across the fens
and I did as far as childhood would allow, to the
worlds end. That day I walked and walked and
walked and stopt to eat some sorrel and went on
walking till the sun had dropt behind the elms
and the men from the Bluebell came in search of
me and I was all of four mile from home and
when I was home again and we in bed you askt
me little sister what the worlds end were like
and I started to tell you but you were asleep by
then more worn out with worry than I with my
walking. You never see me here, little sister,
none of you. Not you nor Mary Joyce none
of you.

I have been thinking that there was a time
when I could see the whitethorn, touch it taste it
smell it and not think on Richard Turnills
coffin. There was a time when it was all I
needed to think on Mary Joyce. I could think of
her, I could smell the smell of May and think of
her. Always when I was walking from market or
out on the fens or rhyming my rhymes or
working in a garden I would think of her. I
hated the sameness of gardens. It cloyed me but I
were away from it inside my head and thinking
of Mary Joyce. Why do you not come and see
me and bring her with you.

John Clare

You may think parts of his letter strange but I do not and you would not if you read the other letters that have come in the years of late. There is light in this letter, more light than there had been in anything for a long, long time. Too little light, perhaps, and now too late, but something to brighten the memory. And, you know, his thinking of Richard again and expressing those thoughts to me is something I treasure, I cannot deny that to you.

This letter is the last I shall receive from him, his last of all, I think, and is so much happier than anything else that I associate with him in the seven years since we met face to face the final time. I had travelled to Northampton with my husband to visit John and we sat together, the three of us, on a bench in the yard of the asylum there. John talked a great deal, sometimes of things I understood and sometimes as though he were a bare-fist fighter awaiting a match, in a coarse tongue. The visit was drawing to a close and I was content that there was some sense, perhaps a greater deal than I had hoped for, yet in his head. We were saying our farewells when he spoke very tenderly and said: 'I have always had a great love for you, little sister, you have always been the one to whom I was closest. Let me kiss you.'

I waited for the touch of his lips on my cheek but he walked past me towards an inmate, a tall and red-haired man who had been loitering about while we had sat and talked, and kissed this man most delicately upon the cheek and walked off in his company, the man following slightly behind John, subserviently, it seemed to me.

My husband, who had sat throughout the interview in silence, became most insistent that we should leave immediately. 'This visit was a mistake,' he said. 'The man is demented in his insanity.'

I never showed my husband the occasional letters that came for me from John in the time since then. They would merely have confirmed him in his opinion. And I have never shown him that last letter. To me it is a clear flow of remembrance and peace. My husband would demean the letter and its importance to me by pointing out the flaws in its construction and logic. He could not see beyond them. He cannot see.

But this letter, these memories, are small comfort and throw little by way of relief on the sombre dusk that lies around my life. For some there is the hope that loved ones whom they have lost will come again, out of that dimness to meet them and be the friends they were. I see nothing of that hope in the darkness I speak of, nothing that promises even the least crack in the black façade. I may dream, on nights when the storms blow outside my home, of Richard Turnill stopping at my gate but I know he will never come inside my door and I know that if I were to walk out there he would be gone – I mean his imagined person, for that, I know, is all he is.

There is no hope in the darkness.

And there is no hope, even now, of the darkness that fell between John and me lifting or fraying. It was always there and it will always be there. Perhaps because, like his hardness towards our father, he wanted it there. Perhaps there was nothing I could do to lighten it. I do not know, I can honestly say that to you, and nothing will ever bring an answer to me now.

On days when the shadow seems to cover the whole of my world I think his kissing of the inmate, in my name, was another way of thickening the shade between us. Not that he was aware of that, I am sure, but his mind, even in its demented state, was telling him that I was not the sister he had been born closest to. She was dead. His other breathing half was dead and I could not replace her. But I try, God knows I try, to keep those days and that terrible feeling as distant as death.

II
Patty Clare

*H*E TOLD ME THE FIRST TIME he ever seed me was one Sunday at the Flower Pot. You may believe that or not but it seems a likely thing to me. The Flower Pot were an inn where John would sometimes fiddle and I would sometimes walk to with my father. It were rare enough for me to be there of a Sunday and rarer still for him but that Sunday it fell that we were there together. He could tell me every mite of that day. What I wore and what I said and how I looked and what way my hair were but I have no remembrance at all of how the day went with me and much less and none at all the way John was. I can't recall even the sight of him. He might as well not have been there at all for ought I knew of him. But there he was and he was completely taken by me. I had no notion of this until a great time afterward. He didn't tell me for months and months what had happened that afternoon. It seems, according to his recollection, that when the dancing and music come to an end everyone set out for home and he dawdled, waiting to see which way my father and me should walk. But while he was waiting a man from Helpston come and asked him if he knew the tune of some song or other, and when he got himself free again we were gone from the yard. He told me as how he climbed a tree, right up into the topmost branch, and searched the lanes about until he caught sight of the figures of my father and me walking homeward. He stayed in the branch till we were out of sight and he had settled his mind as to which way we had gone. But by the time he had come down to earth again the inn were shut and not a soul about to ask our names of. So he were left as badly fixed, he said, as if he hadn't known the road we took at all. He knew the road but not the name and no one there to ask of.

But that were a start, he said. Knowing, at least, the path I'd took and the one I were likely to be found upon another time. He said he conjured names for me all the way back home that evening. And never once come up with Patty, my true name. Well, not my right true name. My given name were Martha but I never heard it used in my hearing, neither as child or woman, apart from when the vicar called it from the altar and we marrying. But in that I'm jumping over much in the way of us.

The second time I met with John I do remember rightly. I were out walking the fens one summer evening. It must have been high summer for the flies were clouding out the shelters of the trees and I had on a light dress for the weather. I were walking a path for sport, not thinking of any place I might go but going where the path might take me, when I come face to face with John. He weren't striking to look at, not at first. A short, wild-haired man even then. He were carrying his fiddle and bow under his arm, wrapped in a kerchief. For all I knew this was the first time we had met. I did not recall him playing among the other fiddlers in the Flower Pot. But he remembered me. I would have passed on along my way with a nod or a 'good morrow' had he not set to talking as soon as he were near me.

'I remember you from the Flower Pot,' he said at once.

I were silent.

'You were there a month ago, one Sunday. Dancing.'

I nodded, wondering all the while if I should

remember this man for some good reason. He told me then who he was and what he had been about at the Flower Pot and how he had noticed me among the other girls. He didn't tell about his climbing into the tree to watch me go but he did tell me I was the prettiest girl he had met in all his time. Not that I believed him. I'd seen enough of girls and heard enough of men to know it were not true for myself, but still, it were nice to think that he might say it.

He lingered talking. He were on his way to some alehouse or other to play but he took his time in talking. He asked my name and I told him it were Patty. And then he told me how he had tried to find it in his heart, my name in his heart, in walking home from the Flower Pot.

'And did you hit on Patty?' I asked.

'No,' he said, 'not Patty, but almost every other name.'

He stayed to talking so long that his fiddling fell by the wayside. We stood there in that one spot till the flies and midges took their wing in the dusk and there were only we two left there, giggling and gossiping together. Afterwards, I will confess, I wished he had done more than talk but that wasn't a complaint I was to have for very long. When it came to lovemaking, once he had made his bed in that direction, he were happy to lie in it as often as chance would allow. And so was I. But that is not to say we fell to love that first of our evenings together. No indeed, that was a most honest evening with only banter between us.

He left me to the top of my path that night. It were dark as the heart of a blackberry, not a moon from one end of the night to the other, and he walked to the sight of my home. I wouldn't let him come no further for fear my father should be rambling about. Not that he had anything to say against me walking with boys but at the time I were strong with a shoemaker from Olney and my father thought he would be a good match for me. I knew John would get a poor look in if my father had his way and thought it better to pick a time of my own making to take him into the light. Soon enough, I thought. Let's see what kind of lad he first turns out to be and then we'll see how far he may be took. He were good to talk with and laugh with but I were not about to say no more than that. Not until I could be sure of him.

He told me afterwards that on the night as he first walked me home he could not find his way back to his own house, what with the darkness and not being certain of where he were in the first place, and he wandered about until well into the night and still got no nearer to any path that he might know. In the end he lay down in a dyke and pulled his coat as well about him as he might and fell to sleep as though the earth beneath him were a softer mattress than his own.

He were always a one for sleeping out if the night overtook him on his walks. I didn't find that easy when I first knew him. If he could find a dry spot, be it winter or summer, he would sleep as sound as a black cat in the chimney seat. No wind or rain or snow would disturb him if the place were dry. He seemed wrapped up in his own warmth. I saw him nights with only a shirt to keep the cold out and he would still be snug within himself.

He wrote a verse for me, the first night we talked. 'Of all the days in memories list' it went, but I were never a one for verses or reading. I could not read then and cannot.

He said the verses over to me and they sounded well enough. There were other verses, too, with my name in them and he would read them to me or say them out of his head. I had never met a man who would risk being laughed at by saying what he had writ. But John did. I will admit it took me time to take him with any seriousness. I knew men and the rambles they will take to get you in the bramble bush and this were just another way, as far as I could see at first. But bit by bit I took to believing he had writ the words and that they had some feeling in them. What woman would not, for few women, or men, want other than to believe the one who talks of love to them? Is that not true? I know it is.

I would get John to go back to that first verse because

it held some feeling for me that nothing afterwards, no matter how well it sounded, could hold. 'Of all the days in memories list . . .' Even yet I like to say that over to myself. I suppose there is no great beauty in it. I've heard so many folk talk of this poem and that of John's, I've sat and listened to all kinds of talk in our home about the merits of his work, but I hold that line most closely in my heart.

Not, let me say, that I were the only one in his life. Not even that I thought I were. I knew how to lead a handful of men in the one long dance and I knew just as well when I were one of many dancing on another's hand. I made my own enquiries about John. I knew a good many people out the Helpston way. News and wind travel fast and news is often faster.

He were walking evenings up the woods and standing there, among the trees, gaping down on the house of Mary Joyce. I could see no purpose in doing that, for it were an aimless task. He could never walk down and talk with her, not in her father's yard. There were always a why and a wherefore for his being there in the woods. He were listening for some particular chelp. He could herry there for hours on end without no reason other than the hope that she would pass across the yard or stand for a moment at her door, and most often there was not even that. He told me once she were pretty as a rainbow, though I never seed her myself. Others as did said she was not the beauty that he made her out to be. But then that were John. I were not the beauty he made me out to be neither.

But it weren't just Mary Joyce. Indeed, she were the least of worries in one way, though the greatest in another. But there were others a plenty. Some I knew of and some I didn't.

There was Betty Sell, across the fen. Her I did know to see and hear. A tossy sort of girl that I never took to. But I know he were lying with her the same time as he were lying with me. When he were with me I wouldn't think of her, but when he were away lime-burning I would know he were with her. It may have been that it were a race between her and me, we both of us running after him or about him and John standing still to see who would reach him the first. And it may have been that I won because I gave myself all the earlier and found I were with child.

But there, I'm running on in saying that. I must go back. To do him fair and tell the truth I must go back a peg or two.

He told me things as you wouldn't expect a man to say. Some things were not what anyone would want repeated about them but he would tell me straight and fair. He told me of times when his neighbours would gather at the Blue Bell, of a summer evening, and call him as he passed and have him sit and read his verses over to them, asking him for more and more and leading him along like a blinded cauf. And then they would laugh at him and put new words and twists and meanings into the words he had writ.

But they weren't the worst, he said. The worst were those he knew as pretended to liking what he wrote. Men who told him to his face as how good his writing was and how much they would do to help. I come to know these people myself, or others like them, by and by.

He told me too, a good many years afterwards, as how he had wrote verses for Mary Joyce but had been afeared to read them to her, she being of farm stock and him being what he was. He would stand in the woods, he said, and recite them down like rain upon her roof top. He would carry the verses in his pocket in the hope of meeting her on the road or at Stamford market and would come home downcast because he had not seen her.

It were made all the harder, he said, by the memories of a time when he and she had walked from school together, had played together as children, had been in one another's confidence. Now that he needed it, he said, it was not there. And once or twice when he did meet her face to face in the street of a market day, even if she were alone, he would finger the paper in his pocket and count to a number, telling himself he would give the verses to her, but he never did. He didn't even speak, he said.

I couldn't understand of that. 'If you had something to say,' I'd tell him, 'then why be put off by her standing. You have never been slow in talking with me,' I'd say.

'But that is different,' he'd say and leave it lie at that.

Sometimes, I thought, I ought not to have listened to his talk of her but I were trying to understand and make some sense on it for him as well as me. I believed the best that could be done for all on us was to hear out what he had to say and answer it myself. I'm not sure now that that was so but I'm not sure neither that it wasn't.

The same water can't be drunk twice so leave it be.

There's many things like that I've left unturned this good long time. There was nothing to be got from turning them but pain and that comes easy enough without us going out to find where it has nested. And he told me other things as well. Things I might be better not to tell you at all.

Still, if the worst were told, then there's as much reason for telling the best as well, no doubt. He'd whisper things to me in the dark or he'd say them out straight, out loud in the evening and we walking. Out as bold as Beauchamp in the white of day, with the sun still shining and nothing to spare his blushes or mine. And we sheltering beneath a tree, he'd say something that set me hot as soon as it were said. We'd be there waiting for the dusk to make our loving respectable and, of a turn, we couldn't wait that long, neither on us. We'd fall to kissing and he'd touch me, his hand beneath my blouse, his fingers like another tongue, licking the skin of my belly and up and down from there.

But there. I were courting a shoemaker when first I met our John. I'll say nothing more than this. He were a right dry stick — it's not the first time I've said that and it won't be the last.

And then I started taking John to home and there were nothing said the first and second time. My father were used to seeing lads about the place. But when he started calling night after night my father were not in the smallest way pleased. Not that he said anything direct, he were too foxy for that.

'Whatever happened with that shoemaker?' he'd say.

'Too busy with his trade,' I'd say and pass him off like that.

But he come back to that, as soon as he got wind that John and me were more than two peas waiting for the pod to burst. The pods were well burst by then, if only he had known. He wouldn't laugh to hear me say that, God rest his soul, but it is true.

'That other lad,' he'd say, 'that lad that come here courting you, he had a trade, he had good prospects. What has this Clare? Nowt.'

I understood my father saying this. He never had a brass farthing himself. He worked hard and long but that brought nothing to his life but another year of work and another year again, as far back and as far forward as he could see. He wanted more than that from lads as might have an eye on me. He were keen to see me wed to a tradesman. He were keen to see me contented, too, but his mind told him contentment come with shillings on the table at the end of a day's working. He would never hear of me saying how dry the shoemaker were. I would never dare to say it to him. It would be breath gone out on the wind when it might as well have been saved for talk of something else. But a dry stick is what he were and John were the one for words and whisperings and feelings.

He'd talk and talk about the woods and the flowers and the fens and it were like a river gabbling on, with music coming unexpected from everything he said. He might be talking on about something or other, about the swallow, say, telling me the differ between the male and female, talking quite the same as any time.

'Look,' he'd say, 'the chestnut colour on the male is deeper than the female and his tail is longer – thinner, too.'

And then, without as much as drawing breath, he'd drop his voice and whisper to me and his mouth would slip between my breasts. And other places, if I tell you the truth. He would pleasure me, out there in the lanes or on the fens or in the trees beyond the church, and one thing must be said, the pleasuring did not end on our wedding day. He were never content unless I were.

Let me tell you, I can recall nights, winter and summer, outside our door and me backed up against our wall and John upon his knees before me and – well, all I'll say is this, I'd bite on the end of my petticoat to keep from crying out from the rapture of what John did to me. His tongue would travel down the side of my neck and trace a river between my breasts and then he'd be there upon his knees, his face buried in the folds of my dress and his hands working slowly from the tops of my boots, sliding slowly up my legs, my skirt rising with them until he had found his way to where he was wanting. And then his tongue would work between my thighs, damply, damply finding its way to where I was most content to have it. But contentment isn't what I were feeling, not for long. His tongue would lick and push and lick and push until I bit my petticoat between my teeth to keep from screaming with joy, lest my father come outside.

I tremble to think what he might have made of that sight, me against the wall, John upon his knees, his face buried between my legs and me moaning with the rising heat that was flowing from his tongue.

Even now it makes me warm to think of that and of

all the places he would do that, or the like, to me. On gravestones, in our yard, out on the fens, in Burghley Park beneath the trees, in his mother's kitchen, once, when she were expected any time. I were sitting in a chair, a night in winter, and the place were empty as the sky, apart from him and me. He were sitting there across from me, writing, and he dropped his pencil and bent to pick it up, and before I knew it his head were there. And I began to feel myself slipping away and still I was all the time thinking I heard his mother's step outside. Listening and not wanting to hear. And him murmuring into me, telling me how much he loved that part of me, talking and kissing all in one. And then I heard the scrape of his mother's boots but he went on until the latch cracked. He turned and pushed a log into the fire and dropped my skirts about my legs and smiled, all in one instant, the same instant as his mother pushed the door. I sat there, terrified and delighted. Wet with fear and excitement. That were John. He might do that three times in a night before I could get my chance to do the same for him.

And then, they say, in marrying you find your own place and your own quietness. But there were nights when I bit on my nightgown to keep his father and his mother from hearing. And later still I'd do the same for fear the children would be roused from their sleep by my happiness.

It's no lie to say I missed all that for many a year after he were gone. I miss it still, I don't mind saying so. That were the purest pleasure I have ever had. The purest. But there were other things. Other, slower pleasures from our lives.

He'd sit, from time to time, and list his books. I liked to hear him do that. To hear him read the names: *Abercrombies Gardener's Journal; The Seasons*; and *Paradise Lost*. That one he were most particular and proud of as he'd bound it himself. He took satisfaction in a thing like that and I took satisfaction in his contentment about that kind of thing.

But all of this came later and I'm running on again. And we courting, he would come to see me of an evening whenever he could, and when I'd see him in the lane or across the fen, I'd run and catch my clean gingham and take it from the bush and put it on, dry or not. Oh, the joy of waiting for a glimpse of him in the lane, some flower or branch or other swinging in his hand, his hair blowing back and his head bobbing about to some song he had made. And his smile at seeing me.

And it wasn't that I was waiting for the deeper delights of the night. I were pleased at his coming, pleased to see him in our yard, happy at the sight of him. We'd go walking out across the countryside, his arm about me, his face turning this way and that so that his voice would come from everywhere. Sometimes he'd bury his face in my hair and whisper and I'd think the whisper came from inside my own head and he'd say some words I was longing to hear and I'd wonder whether he had been listening, his ear against my skull, so that he could hear the things I were thinking about him. It often looked that way to me.

We'd walk to the villages or along the fens but he'd never take me into the woods. They were full of mantraps, he'd say, for poachers. He told me as how he was walking back home one night after fiddling in some alehouse and he heard a man in the woods.

'He were screaming and screaming,' John said to me. 'I knew what part of the wood he were in but I were afraid to go in myself. I heard a good time afterwards as he had his leg cut off.'

Another man would make excuses for not going in but John told his fear. 'I were afraid,' he said.

It were the same all over, trees felled, lands enclosed and ploughed. 'The heart torn out of the land,' as John had it. But it weren't just his fear that burned in him. He were full of anger, too, at the thought of what were happening to the countryside. It weren't that he thought it more his right nor anyone else's but only that he had always rambled the fens and gone about the woods as he had liked. Him and all his childhood friends had grown to manhood in the belief that the land were there for all. Some might have their names upon a part of it and some might use a part of it and some might never own a part of it, but it were there for the use of all and the enjoyment of all.

I sometimes thought the pleasure that John gave me were like the pleasure he took from the countryside. He never said as much, and I'm not a one for making out my own ways of taking what our life was or wasn't for, but that one thing I do believe. His pleasure flowed into me and the pleasure of the fens flowed into his lifetime, man and boy. There must be something in that, I believe. And to have that taken from him, to be told and told again where and where not to walk, to wake up one day and find a fence about a wood as you were used to walk through, that is a bitter thing. Just the way it were for me to find myself without the warmth and closeness and pleasure, yes the pleasure, I were used to, that too was a bitter thing.

John were due his ramblings in the fields and I were due him in me when I wanted him but neither on us got our due. They tried to lock up the pastures and the trees, or worse, they pulled them down, and then John locked himself away from me and I were left with nothing, no one in my bed. I know the loss he felt for I felt as much and more in losing him. He could see his woods and his fens and could not go into them. I could see him and not be able to rely on him. The woods were there but out of his reach. He were there, not dead, but out of reach of me and his children.

He had his anger about all of that. He were a man who were angered by the hurt of anything. I seed him run at men twice his size as were badger-baiting. Run at them without a care for how he come out of it. But then he were gone from me and there were no one I could run at. I couldn't scream at him and call him the bastard son of a bastard, as I sometimes did when I were angered by his going-on. He had his angers but he knew who they were intended for and at the least he had the satisfaction of spending them. I had nothing. I couldn't shout at the children. It weren't them as was to blame. I couldn't shout at him, locked up them miles away. And all the people as had sung his praises and told us how great our lives were going to be were long gone once the troubles came to roost. There were no one left but me to turn my anger on, not one, and that was even greater cause for anger in the end. The real bitterness is gone now, or all but, still I remember it without having to dig too far.

Not that his going was a new thing to me. When we was walking out together he disappeared as well. He thought that I were carrying and he got drunk and went off to enlist in the artillery. To escape. The sergeant laughed at him, told him he were too short and too weak and sent him home again as soon as he'd arrived.

He crept back to Helpston as timid as he ought and he come up about our house a week later and smiled a feeble smile and tried to laugh the whole thing off. But I were having none of it.

'Keep away from me,' I told him. 'See how the artillery keeps you amused at night.'

He tried to tell me it had all been meant for the best, to get some money for him and me and any child that we might have.

'Who said anything of children?' I said.

He weren't sure as to what my circumstances were and I weren't about to tell him until such time as I were sure myself.

'And anyway,' I said, 'you might have told me where you were and what you were about, running off to join the army.'

'I were drunk,' he said. 'I wouldn't have done it otherwise.'

'There was nights when you were drunk with me,' I said, 'but that never stopped you finding your way to where you wanted to be and it never stopped you telling me what it was you wanted to do to me.'

He had nothing to say to that.

'It's the day after the fair,' I said and left him standing where he were and flounced inside and shut our door.

When he come back, three or four days later, he had verses and a ribbon for me and news that he were working. At lime-burning, the far end of the fens. I were happy to see him and happy to hear of his work, though

I wouldn't have been had I knowed he would meet Betty Sell through living off across the fen. I know he were lying with her and I can only think that he used some of his charming ways to get inside her thighs, just as he had done with me. I don't blame her or him but it were something I could never prove and something I knew right well, from knowing him. No doubt he had her up against a wall or on her back behind some house or in his bed for all I know. In the end, she were luckier. Or not. Or not.

It were a wet and dreary March and we marrying. He were disinclined to marry me. I knew that, without his having to say as much. I knew he were. You cannot lie with someone, give yourself to them night after night, hear them talk of things you would not dare to mention to yourself and still not know how they feel. That were how I knew of Betty Sell and that were how I knew he did not want to marry me. Oh, he came and listened to me and said he should look after me and the baby but he were disinclined to marrying.

I recall the night he said we should be wed. My father took him into our kitchen and they sat drinking. I went walking to a neighbour's house, as I had been told by my father, and stayed there until close to midnight and when I come back John told me we were going to be wed. He were drunk and my father were half-drunk but my father were smiling and John were not. He were easily made drunk but he weren't happy and neither were I. I did not like to see him so and I had no wish to marry him if it were only for the sake of keeping one name for the child, to call it Clare instead of Turner. I would not do that to John. I were too fond of him for that.

I had been angry with his running off to join the army and I were angry when I thought of Betty Sell and him. But there were others, too, I might have felt a bitterness about. Mary Joyce, who was always on his lips. Elizabeth Newbon. He had been courting her when he met me and I didn't reckon as he had dropped her just to walk with me, not when he could walk with both of us, at least a while. All these angers and doubts but nothing as would make me want to trap him because I were carrying.

To see him there with my father on our kitchen floor, and my father full of loud laughter and slapping John upon the back and saying as how we could sleep easily now and not be worrying about what might come in the way of children, was no joy to me. John were drunk but that had not made him any happier. Even the drink had not dulled his mind to what he had done.

Not that he did not want me, I can say that. It were what he were leaving behind. And what he were bound to once he crossed the church door. Bound to keeping wife and family and knowing family were just begun. I felt for him in spite of all. I knew we should both have liked a better start than this, but there you are. There were nothing we could do. No way to put the fire out.

I recall, as John were leaving that night, my father said as he might stay if he so wished.

'You might as well lie with your wife tonight as any night,' he said. 'There's nothing that can happen now as hasn't happened yet.'

He was laughing and urging him to stay and not to venture out into the darkness and the rain. John were standing near the fireplace and he reached down and I saw him close his hands about a stool as we had there, about the leg, and I were certain he would bring it down upon my father's head or smash it on the floor. The more my father laughed the more it seemed that John would not contain his anger.

'I think that John wants to tell his father and mother,' I said. 'I think he wants to get back home.'

My father nodded and slapped him on the back again and bade him goodnight.

I walked with John a good part up the lane. It were cold and the rain were falling and we stood under the hedge and I held his face and told him straight.

'You haven't made a pledge to me,' I said. 'You've spoken with my father and I know he got you drunk. Don't think on this as anything you can't go back on.'

And I meant it. I didn't see much good in how he'd

been trapped.

John said nothing. I held onto him. Now it were me holding him, he were the baby being held. I didn't want him to say he wouldn't marry me but I didn't want him doing it to please my father's wishes.

'Do you want me to walk back to Helpston?' I asked him. 'I can, you know, and stay in your house by the fire.'

'No,' he said. 'I shall come and talk with you tomorrow night.'

And then he went off into the darkness.

I stayed where I were sheltered for a good time. I thought perhaps I should never see him again and that would have been a terrible thing but I would have taken it in place of John being unhappy all his life.

When I went back inside my father smiled at me and winked.

'You were a good time out there,' he said. 'No harm in that.'

I took the stool in my hands, the stool nearest the fire, and flung it against the wall. It crashed in pieces across our floor but I didn't care. I felt a good deal better for having done it.

When John come back the next evening he had told his mother and his father and his sister. I had expected, if he came, that he would still be angry but it seemed as he had set his heart on this and there were no more to be said.

In spite of all, I think John's expectations were that we should be unhappy. I think, at the start, he saw no hope for us beyond the pleasures of our company and the coming of the baby. That did not stop him going through with the marriage and it did not mean he did it with a bad grace. It meant only that he set himself to live without the certainty of happiness in his marriage.

But we were not unhappy. I don't say life were always like a summer day but we were a good deal, a great deal, more happy than most people as we knew. And a great deal happier than I had hoped we should be. Maybe that come of neither of us having hopes beyond the way things were. We expected little and anything what came were a blessing and little by little we built on that. Don't think I'm saying there was never things that went awry and never times when I felt hard done by, even before he went that final time, but all in all things went as well as might be hoped for.

We lived with his parents. His father were well battered by the time of our wedding. He were worn out with too many long days in the rain and too many hours of work that barely fed him. John always said as there was nothing of his father in him but I think, and I've never said this afore John, that part of what wore out Parker Clare were the same kind of despair and loss that wore out his son, but at least in John we saw it clearer.

On top of that, John's mother were struck with the dropsy, so when we come to live in their home it were less than I might have liked. I hoped, as all brides do, to have our own cottage and our own garden and our own place to be together, to make our own home as we would have it ourselves. Instead of that I were trying to make a home for us and keep a home as John's mother had made it. And I did. I kept the room as clean as a woman could. And when in time we had our own cottage it were cleaner than any house or cottage or manor in the parish. No matter who were coming or at what hour, our home were clean and tidy. You ask anyone.

And I were there for John in any need. I were there for him to talk with and there for him to spend himself inside and there to hush the children when he were in need of quiet.

One time, a good time after John had been taken, I were walking back from Stamford, and Morgan the carpenter's wife overtook me and we got to talking. She asked as how our John were and I told her what I could.

'I always thought how well you went together,' she said. 'I had no notion, when you come to live here, how you might go but I often think about you and him, in the days when he were here.'

I had never thought she even passed a word on me and I told her so.

'Indeed I did,' she said. 'In the start I would see the two of you at odd hours, out walking the fens or up by the spinney. I recall one morning, at dawn, I saw you come arm in arm out of the fog and both on you looking at nothing but each other, and I thought how happy you seemed. It were the morning of our Ellen's wedding and I were up preparing and I thought if only she were to be as happy as you two how lucky she would be and how blessed.'

I smiled at her and she saw the tears in my eyes.

'At least you have that to keep,' she said to me. 'At least you have something to go back on. Some have nothing to remember all their lives.'

And I did. That day I sat in our kitchen and looked at the garden as he had made and across at the pastures he rambled over and the trees he were so fond of all his life.

I saved him for as long as I were able. I gave him as much of me as I could and I gave him as much of himself as I knew how to find. And towards the end, before he were gone, I would sit with him when I could and listen to his talking or just sit with him for companionship. I should like to have had some cure but I had none and so I sat with him. I'd lay down beside him and hug him. What more could I do? I still hug him to me when I can, even at this distance. I stop in the garden or when I'm here in this kitchen alone and try to picture him as he were. Not as a young man but as the man as needed love and holding when last I saw him and I put my arms around that picture and try to keep him warm, whatever he's doing where he is now. I still sit by him when I'm sat here alone. I can only hope he knows that. But I have no way of knowing.

Once, I could turn his head, he would climb a tree to watch me, and I hope my love can turn him round again. I haven't bid hope goodbye, not yet. I've tried to keep my love as true as I can and hope that something will reach him. Though, God knows, I can't imagine how.

I think of us crossing the pastures in the evening, walking through the ghosts of sheep, and him softly singing to me, some love song as he had made for me, some words that were like the west breeze, that soft and that warm. And I'd ask him to lay down beside me and I'd guide him until I were satisfied and then I'd satisfy him. And we'd lie there, looking up through the trees, up through the sycamore keys, at the last of the light in the sky. And then we'd go on walking, arms about one another, close. I loved him that much. I never wanted any of that to end.

Now, when I go back across them ways, changed and all as they be, I keep meeting his ghost and my ghost, arm in arm, my head on his shoulder, his hands in my hair, his kiss on my breast. But now I walk alone.

One time, and he going off to work somewhere, he left me a letter on our table. I could not read it then but years after I asked our Eliza to tell me what it said. And bit by bit, in learning it and going over the letters, I have got to know the words.

I have it here, look. It says:

Dearest Patty,

I have wrote this poem to keep you close by me and I away. You will know it sometime when you need knowing.

How sweet can courting prove
How can I kiss my love
Muffld i' hat and glove
From the chill air
Lay by thy woolen vest
Rap no cloak oer thy breast
There my hand oft hath prest
Pin nothing there
There my head drops to rest
Leave its bed bare.

John Clare

Isn't that what the letter says? I have that and some days it means a great deal to me to have it and some days it seems such a paltry piece of paper to have at the end of all of this.

Oh, there were signs and signs. As far back as the autumn after we were wed. That October John's father fell ill and come close to dying. And his apple tree were barren that same year. People laugh at me when I point to that as the worst sign of all but John were forever telling me as how that tree had been their saving many a time and now I seen it barren, the same time as his father was ill, and I thought it all pointed to no good coming. I still say that were the first real sign. And that tree never bore again, as true as I may breathe. We were left to fend for ourselves and for John's father and mother. It didn't seem a laughing matter then to me and it still don't.

And then the thing as should have been a source of gladness and of us being able to live a better life, John's writing, brought its own trouble in its wake. Not that I were not happy to see him rising in the eyes of those who know of these things, but they were not interested in John or me, not in the most part. They were interested in what he wrote for what it might mean to their own lives and fortunes. Not all on them but most.

There were always someone coming to see him. Some patron, some publisher, some poet or enquiring traveller as stopped off at our home. I would send one of the children scurrying to Royce Wood, for John would take to writing there if he thought there were visitors upon their way. It might be half an hour before he come lumbering back, and in the meantime I would be answering to the most impertinent questions from these people. There were nothing they would not ask me to tell them about. Nothing. They all but stood at the foot of our bed in the night and watched to see what we might do. It were always where and when and how and why out of their mouths. As if by stopping in they had the right to own us as they might own a piece of cloth.

And then John would arrive and they would set to questioning him and getting him to read his verses and asking what he meant by this and that and always suggesting how his verses might be bettered. There wasn't one who didn't have a better way of saying things than John. If it weren't the way he had writ, it were what he had said or who he had intended the poems for It wore me out and it made him bitter.

They took him off to London to meet with people as I had never heard of – poets and painters and writers. And that in itself were a trial. They promised as he could talk with doctors there about his fits and find a cure for them. That would have been a blessing and a thing worth travelling for.

I recall the day afore he left for London. He come back from Stamford with a new suit. A green suit. A green suit as would make him a laughing stock in Helpston and a suit as had cost him more than he were like to earn in a twelve month. And there were nothing I could say.

'This is what they wear in London,' John told me.

But we weren't living in London. He were going there to meet with people, to talk with publishers and the like, but he were coming back and there were little call for green suits in Helpston, winter or summer.

'Good,' I said to him.

He knew himself the madness in what he had done. I could see that. Walking home from Stamford, mile by mile, it must have worked its way through his brain how crazed he'd been. It didn't need my telling him for him to know. And I said nothing.

He were offered a prospectus to get subscribers for his book of verses. I knew that were what he wanted, more than anything in the world, that were the thing he wanted but he were too much in a muddle to ask people to be his support. He could never go to people and ask them for their money towards the printing of a book and so the notion fell through. But the idea would not go away. He wanted it and his publisher knew how bad he wanted it, until his want drove him to approach people and ask them to subscribe. I seen him come back in here, drained of all strength, more drained than if he'd spent the day out working on the road, drained from the fact of having knocked on people's doors – clergymen and gentry and people as had money left from living – offering them his prospectus and reading them his verse and listening to them telling him how he should change things. Some promised and some criticised and some laughed.

'John Clare, ploughboy poet,' they'd say, laughing. 'I think not.'

But in the end the money come and then the book and then he were all things to all people and we were never done with opening our door to all kinds. And the promises! The promises of books and money and a new cottage and clothes. Oh, the promises as were made under our roof that were never once intended for keeping. I could cut through them when I think as what they did to us.

I do believe and believe it rightly that they were as much to blame for putting him away as were any of his sicknesses in his head or his fits and turns in childhood. All the promises made on this very floor and the only one as was kept was to take him off to London and fill his head with thinking he were like the rest of them writers and painters and suchlike, so that he come back here unhappy, wanting to be somewhere else and something else and he were never happy afterwards. Telling me that he knew not how to behave in London but I could see he were not content no more with being with us. Not if the truth were told.

He were always one for wandering but I knew that afore I married him and I were prepared for his goings. But always I knew where he were. He were never more distant than Barnack or Wittering and that were the furthest he would roam. And I knew he would be back. If he slept out a night he would be back by the end of the next day. But from the time they set his mind on other things he were never rightly here, even and he sitting in the corner there, he were away some other place and in a different set of life than we could hope to live.

And always there were the money. It had a place afore it come to us at all. It were waited on for his mother or his father or the children or books or something.

There were no hope in his writing. The books were there and the knocks on the door and him being paraded from place to place in his green suit and days when he believed in all of that and days when it were all I could do to keep his eyes off the bottom of the pit.

And after all the talking stopped we were left with nothing and he turned a second time to lime-burning. He were away again, the far end of the fen, staying in a house with other men as were working at the lime-burning too. A coarse lot they were, by John's account.

He would come back when he could and tell me stories. Once, he told me, one night, a traveller come from London and lodged with them under the same roof. They filled the man's head with tales of all the travellers as some of them had killed. They told him that three of them had cut the throats and robbed the purses of travellers on the fens. This unfortunate man were

afeared to travel on, being certain as he should be next
to die if he ventured outside of the door, certain that he
should have his throat sliced and his purse stole and his
body thrown in a ditch. And he were afeared to sleep,
thinking they should come and cut him where he lay.
So he sat by the fire and every time a man snored upstairs
he jumped and looked about. He were gone afore
dawn, afore they rose for work. They laughed and
laughed about him. Thinking of him sitting by the
hearth all night long, jumping at every snore, and them
sleeping quite content.

He would tell me stories such as that and I would
listen and laugh and think that Betty Sell might again be
in his head but he never mentioned her and I would
not ask.

He worked hard at the lime-burning. He worked and
slept and saved. And if he did see Betty Sell it did not
stop him thinking of us. He saved all of fifty shillings.
And then one night, while he slept, it were took from
his coat by the same men as worked and ate and lodged
with him. Hail-fellow-well-met and then taking fifty
shillings from his coat. What we could have done with
that! But we seemed, or John seemed, to meet with folk
like that all his life.

In the end, between the work and the company he
were forced to keeping and living with, and the loneliness,
his loneliness, he come back here. He were a great one

for going off with notions about how things would be and what would come of them but he always needed something to come back to. That were one of the pains of his finally going. I thought he should be most unhappy with not having anything of the places and people he loved about him. But he has found some kind of contentment and that is the greatest sickness in him, the greatest change, that he has found a life away from the life that were so important to him. To be out there in a life of his own, without a single trace of anything from here, and yet not to seem to miss it.

But going back. He threw up the lime-burning and come back to working at the Blue Bell. He took in and out the barrels and suchlike and he were treated well enough. But bit by bit the work become a different kind of work and he found himself out at all hours, morning and night, taking care of cattle, running errands, tending to everything as needed tending to. And of course he nodded aye to everything as he were asked to do and then come grumbling here to me.

'Why don't you grumble where you should?' I'd say. 'There's nowt I can do to change the work as has been given. Talk to him as can.'

But he would not.

There were another fellow working in the Blue Bell as was supposed to help him, Samuel Foot were his name, but he spent his days in talk and John went on with the work. And long after John had left that work Samuel Foot were still there. 'Tis true what they say, creaking doors hang the longest.

'Say something,' I'd tell him.

'No, there's nothing to be gained from that,' he'd say.

I thought it were all of a kindness but I heard it said, and I cannot say from who, and said to me, that there were another reason for his putting up with Samuel Foot. It seems he had a sister, Ann, and she would come and visit him and he working and John and her took a great liking of one another. My informant told me as how him and Ann would go out together at every opportunity and meet in the nights and once, or so I'm told, they were come across together, lying in the woods, and they were not there for looking at the stars or trees. Not in the way as they were found. I did not hear that till a good time afterwards and by then Ann Foot had moved to live in Northampton and were married to a mason there.

And talking of Northampton, John would go there on business for the Blue Bell and stay over a night and he met up with Mary Ludgate and he there. But that come to my ear much quicker and I soon put a bucket on that fire. I were waiting for him and he come back one dull, wet, miserable January day. He come in expecting food and fire and a cosy hearing but I told him straight out as how he could turn about and walk back the way he'd come and try to find some comfort in her as he had spent the night with in Northampton. He could not guess as how I knew and he went on about that, not denying what he'd done but wanting to know where I had heard this from.

'How I heard or what I heard or who from is not what matters,' I told him. 'What matters is what you were at. Tell me you didn't lie with her, tell me you didn't make her moan and groan when she come with you. Tell me that.'

He stood there, the rain dripping off the end of his coat, for all of Christendom like a beaten dog. I left him waiting for his supper and, I can tell you, he waited a good time afore he found my porches open to his knock. And that cured him for a while, as least as far as I were to know. And he going to Northampton he would tell when he would be back and what he had to do. The following time as he went he took Eliza with him and the time after that he walked straight back through the night and there he were at the table when I woke in the morning.

And still, all this time, they'd come in carriages and on horseback. Wanting to see him, dragging him from his work, having him recite for them. How many times did I send for him from work to come and perform for some loud person as had only suggestions for improvement and then went off without as much as a thank you. As if John owed it to them to perform.

'Why do you do it for them?' I'd say.

'There might be something at the end,' John would say. 'When it comes to publishing another book.'

One man, I remember, come back four times and spent above three hours every time. I don't recall his name. He come from Oxford. The first time he listened to John and told him, as they all did, how he could better what he had wrote. The second time he come, one night, and brought his own verse and read it at us above two hours. He come back again the following week with more to read. And when he were going he left a paper wrapped upon the table and we saw him off. I believed it were a guinea or two wrapped up for John's time and trouble and we opened it and he had writ upon the paper.

'What does it say?' I asked John, expecting it were a way of telling him of some good fortune or route as was opening, after all our attention and hospitality.

John laughed but it were not a sweet laugh. 'It says: "God bless you, I shall pray for you." '

The following week the same man come back but this time John got word of his visit and went out and sat in Royce Wood from five o'clock in the evening until after two in the morning and never showed his face. I left our holy friend sitting in his carriage outside our door. He had come in the expectation that John should listen to him perform his greatest work. He did not come again.

But he were only one. The others still came promising. If they had but left us alone I think he might have been content within his mind. But maybe not.

But then our fortune seemed to swing us up into a better place. We was offered a cottage at Northborough. Oh, the joy of moving all our bits to a home of our own. We travelled back and forth the three miles from Helpston to Northborough all that day of our moving, carrying and arranging. Meeting one another at Etton, one coming and one going. And the happiness of the first night under our own roof with no one to think for but us and our children. Our home, our cottage. Oh, how we let our fancy go that night, tired and all as we were. For once I did not think of whether the children might wake. I let my voice cry out with the double ecstasy that I felt, of John in me and us in our own home at last. And yet, that were the most blissful of nights and probably the start of all our troubles and our journey down a road as has never seen the true light of day.

In truth, John never settled in Northborough. We were no more than a good walk from Helpston, but it were like another country to him. The same fens were all about us, Deeping fen and Morris fen. The same rivers flowed, the Glen above us, the Welland to our west, the Nene below us.

'Moreton Leam is still in the same place,' I'd say when he were down.

'I know,' he'd say. No more than that.

But we settled in, John and me and all the children. It were a fine house. A good kitchen and a sitting room as John could use for writing and studying, a back kitchen and three bedrooms. It had been built, at John's asking, with the door facing away from the roadway. He could walk unseen into his garden and orchard and across the fens without as much as notice from those walking the roads. I loved that house. I still do. I spent so long between Walkherd Lodge, where I were born and lived as a girl, and here, as I thought I should never see a home of my own. It were nothing of my doing that John did not settle here. It cannot be that the house were not right. It were the best he had ever lived in and made as much to his order as could have been.

In the years that come after our moving to Northborough we had our better times and less but for John it seemed as though we had moved to the other end of the world. Days and months would go past without anything untoward. His work and writing went apace. He tended his trees and played with the children in the orchard and I kept my garden happy enough and it seemed all were well. But to us, living under one roof with him, there were dykes from which there seemed no escaping for him.

He would take to talking, day after day, as to how he should never have left Helpston, as to how his writing could not prosper away from there. I'd tell him to go back, to stay there a week or two, to write when he were there. Sometimes he would but when he were down there were no urging as could get him out. He would sit in at his table, looking out across the day and seeing nothing in anything. His food would go untouched. The children would not dare to open his door. Even the small ones learned that fast enough. Not that he would beat them, only that he could not be reached, could not be touched even by their frail voices.

And then the world – at any cost his world – went slowly dark and stayed so.

Nothing in it was right. As I have said, he was always talking of London and of how he would be among people there as could understand his gift. And then, on the other side, he would get letters from his publisher and patrons as were telling him of the changes they wanted in his poems.

'They want to publish books over my name but they're not the poems I've wrote,' he would say to me.

And then he would stand in the road and say this same thing to them as were passing. All on that were one matter but then things come to a different pass. He began to complain as how he could not get his poems put into books and he the queen of England's father. In the start I thought he were saying he couldn't get his poems printed even if he were the king but by and by it come clear in talking to us, and about the village, that he were sure in his head that he were born of royal blood.

People would smile at him and then laugh at him in the inn, and the more as they laughed the more upset and enraged he would become. He were like a strange child and they laughed at him as children would.

To remember that time is most painful to me, even at this distance. He were altered, and every day I woke hoping he would have changed back to the way he were but it were not so. He were not the man I had married.

He would still come to me sometimes at night but only in our bed. Never, as he was used to, in the pastures or on the path when we were walking home at night. It were all done quietly now. Oh, he would still bury his face in me, his tongue would still follow its course from my bosom to my belly and down and down and he would still work to bring me pleasure there between my thighs. But when I took his head in my hands and looked at him, his eyes were stone. Black. Dark and hard. No light there, no love, no feeling.

When he kissed me he weren't with me. His mouth were cold. His tongue were not the same as brought me to pleasure a thousand times afore. His hands were touching but there were no feeling in their touch. I were sure that I were lying with a ghost beside me in the dark.

Even in the dawn, when we were holding tight onto each other, just before he would come into me, I'd look for something as I'd remembered from another time, some spark of life, but there were nothing there. Only him moving and moving down into me and nothing in his face at all.

And still he worked and still he wrote his verse and still he spoke with them as come to call on him and still he chased with the children among the apple trees. But he were gone from me.

It come to a time where there were nothing I could do. No one could. The summer were come but it brought no hope. There were doctors come to us and doctors sent their word from London and they said all things were right but I knew otherwise. John were no longer with us, he were somewhere else, out there.

Eliza would walk him across the pastures and back and forth. I would take him with me to Market Deeping. The children would follow him, at a distance, across the fens, for fear of something happening. His sister come and told me about times, and he a boy, when she would come upon him in one of his convulsions. But it were nothing like that now. No fits or turns. It were as like a changeling in our home.

In the end I left him in Eliza's caring one day and walked back to my childhood home to talk with my father about John's condition. And mine.

'You made yourself a hard bed and must lie in it,' he said.

As if I had not lain there long enough to know as much.

'I did not come to ask for anything,' I told my father. 'I come to know what I must do with John.'

'A woman cannot leave her man,' my father said.

I could not make him see as I was not for leaving or breaking the home. I needed someone to tell me where I should turn to find a place for John. My father were no help at all. It had been a day wasted, beyond the pleasure of walking up the summer lane to Walkherd Lodge and remembering my childhood there. When I come back to Northborough I sent again for the doctor and told him as how I saw the changes rung in John. He in turn sent word to John Taylor, as had published John's books, and he, thinking John should come around in time, arranged to have him taken to the care of Dr Allen at High Beach in the Epping forest.

I saw him off, that June day. He were sitting in a coach outside our home, in the very corner, pushed up against the window, though there were no one else upon the seat and only the doctor sitting opposite. I could not kiss him for I had had enough of holding onto him and having nothing of him and so I let him go. 'Twere not that I did not care. I could not care. How could I care and not be taken with him? And so I let him go.

His sister told me once, and I remembered it that day, that when he left them to join the militia his mother and all the village waved him off. There were no one there but me that day. The children were safe away and clear of knowing what were happening. I stood in the open gate and stared at him and then I slammed it shut and went inside and sat and remembered him as he were when first we fell in love. When his hands would hold my waist and his smile were like a light and my tongue would ache after a night of kissing him.

There were some as said I never visited him in High Beach. As though I could up and walk the eighty miles without a care for my children. And if there had been no children to leave, how could I visit him there and live with that again? I sent him word, with John Taylor, that I had not forgotten him and that I should like to visit when I could, lest he think I did not care.

When he come back I asked him what John had said and he would not tell me for a good long time. He said John had smiled and nodded and then he said John had sent his fondest love but all of this did not sound true. I knew that he were lying for he come back without one letter from John. I would not let him leave our home

until he sat and told me what had fallen out on his visit.
And in the end he did.

'When I gave John your message,' he told me, 'he
laughed and laughed in a delirium and then said: "Visit
me! Visit me and I dead." '

I asked John Taylor what this meant.

'He is in a fantasy,' he said. 'He fancies himself to be
Lord Byron. He told me he had watched his own funeral
pass in London, Lord Byron's funeral, with the hearse
and a hundred empty coaches behind and no one there
to see it pass but him. That is what he told me when I
said that you should like to come and visit him.'

And then one July day, with but a few hours'
warning, after years in High Beach asylum, John were
home again, coming in at our door as though he had
been no more than for a long ramble.

His return brought hope but where hope lives fear is
sure to find a home. There were days when our lives and
his would be a pair but there were days when he seemed
to know nothing of what the world is about. He would
return to his talk of being father to the queen of
England, at other times he would swear he was Lord
Byron. He would wander the house in the night,
mumbling and swearing. There was never a peace as
could be counted upon.

It were one evening, one evening in the start of
December, when he finally stopped living here as

husband and father, as himself. I recall each moment.

Eliza had took in a small bunch of wild flowers and put them in a jug on his writing table, knowing how pleased he would be. She were waiting for his coming, to share his happiness. He loved wild flowers always but most especially in the dark days of the year. He often told us how, in several Christmases of his childhood, he had walked up to the high pastures to pick primroses, as out of season as a March apple.

But that December evening he come in and walked through the kitchen without a word and went and sat at his table and shook and shook. I went in after him and pointed the flowers out to him but he didn't seem to see. His eyes were open but he saw nothing and heard nothing. And then he told me that he had been out walking the road when some man, I think he said it were Thomas Brewer, had met him and told him of Mary Joyce's death. In truth, she had been dead above a two year and Eliza had sent the news in writing to John at High Beach but he had never mentioned it in writing back to us.

'But you knew of that. That is done and gone,' I said. He made no sign that he had heard. I left him there and went about my work.

A good time into that night he come out and sat with me and told me as how the Joyces had been cursed once for crossing gypsies, cursed never to have another generation.

'And there she is,' he said. 'Mary Joyce, unmarried, dead.'

The next day he went up through the woods alone and did not come back. I sent the children out to search but they could not find him. I enquired all about and late that night word come that he had been standing about the trees above Glinton Manor, the home of Mary Joyce. He come back some time in the following morning and I sat him down and tried to talk to him. No sense, I thought, in hiding this away.

'Tell me where you were and why?' I said.

And he told me. He started to talk and went on talking in a scramble but bit by bit the tale come out. He told me how her house looked, the high, steep roofs, the chimneys peeping out across the slate, the deep-set porch, the pointed stone. As if he wanted me to see the beauty of the place. And he went on about the windows.

'All the high, fine windows,' he said. 'I stared and stared at them and at the closed curtains of her window and thought of her lying there, her eyes closed as tight as the curtains from the light.'

I listened to all this. I believe he thought she was lying dead in her room that very night. 'But she's long dead,' I said.

He never answered but went on as how her father

would never hear of him being with her, the Joyces being farmers. I knew this were not the same as Betty Sell or all the others. This were something I must hear in the hope of talking it out. And then he turned to me after all that time of not knowing if I was there or not and said: 'Did she think on me? Were I the thought behind her eyes?'

It were from that night as things fell all asunder.

He never went to see where she were laid in the churchyard. It would have been as well if he had done. To see her final end. To see her laid under the sod and clay. To know that she were dead. He never truly faced to that. I urged him to go and see her grave but he never crossed the stile into the church. He said there were nothing there for him. But I think it were her lying there that kept him out. She were dead and he knew it but he would not let himself believe.

It went like that above a week and the darkness hung more and more about him and more and more upon us and about the house. I would not have us all lost in that and I had Eliza send a message to Dr Allen about him going back to High Beach. But that were not to be. Instead, he arranged for John to be took to Northampton asylum.

We kept him with us for that Christmas, the blackest Christmas I ever saw or hope to, and then at the year's end he went from us. He were a good step nearer than

High Beach but no nearer in the end.

There were some, in Northborough and Helpston and Glinton, as said ill of me for not visiting him.

'She never once visited him,' they said.

That and more.

'Him in that asylum for the mad and her not pretending,' they said.

Widow Clare, they called me, some in good nature and some not. But I know this, in spite of all their chattering, I never once refused him in all our life. Not once.

Not since that first time, that first warm evening, a Sunday, when John and me went walking with nothing more than courting in my mind. We walked away beyond the river into a quiet spot and lay down together and kissed and touched and the like. I don't remember what words he said that day but I do remember things as they fell out. A bright summer evening with a deal of folk out on the fens and us together, lying sheltered from them.

I were not one for saying no but neither were I one for hanging myself out like washing for any breeze that blew past. I wanted to do as he asked but he did not ask as others had and neither did he make himself a nuisance as some did. I only knew when it were done that he had taken off my gingham and my blouse and I felt his face against my skin and I thought I might as well be hanging for a sheep as for a lamb. It were as natural and good as that. And never afterwards did I refuse him, not from then. But he were different at that time. We both of us were.

III

Lady Kettering

T IS NOT SO MUCH that I want to justify myself. Not at all. But I consider it important to say what I feel needs to be said. I have heard you talk about the situation on a number of occasions and I am not at all sure that you grasp the truth of the circumstances. I fear you may have been taken in by the well-meant, but inaccurate, accounts offered by Mr Clare's sister and by his wife. They are kind people, kind but somewhat unreliable. And the scene they paint is, like their views on their own lives, equally unreliable.

His sister's marriage, if the truth were openly spoken, is not the path of roses she and her husband would have us believe. And his wife — she likes to call herself Patty but her name is Martha — is not the affable, amiable individual she would like you to imagine. Even that change of name is an attempt to soften the image. I call her Mrs Clare myself; familiarity has a way of turning on the giver, as I shall point out to you. And, let me add, anyone who tries to persuade you that she spent the last twenty years of her life in lonely waiting for a death that would free her from the burdens of this life is lying. I have it on good authority, indeed the best authority, that her life has been by no means one of celibacy.

When Mr Clare first came to my husband, on the recommendation of some petty clerk or other, it was to seek employment of a clerical nature for himself. He waited all day in our kitchen while my husband worked away in his library, oblivious to the presence of the wretched scribbler below. He had been told that the miserable fellow was waiting, but he had forgotten. So it was in so many things in our life. I waited years myself and he seemed to have forgotten that too.

Mr Clare returned home that evening, only to reappear the following morning, still in search of a post. None such existed, of course, but my husband, having heard of his literary endeavours, put a guinea in his hand and bade him God speed. And that was where our paths first crossed. He was clomping noisily down our corridor, his nailed boots clattering on the marble flooring, when I met him. I had no idea whatsoever as to his identity. I enquired about his reasons for being in our house, taking him to be a new man in the garden. He seemed confused by my questioning and said my husband had just dismissed him. I took this to mean that he was leaving my husband's employ and told him he had better quit the house if that was the case.

It was some months later that his work came to my attention, through the efforts of Mrs Emmerson, who had taken him under her ample wing. She invited me to a reading she had arranged and while we awaited his arrival she handed me a letter (I have it still) and asked me to peruse it. It was a roughly written affair that ran thus:

My dear Miss Richardson,

You have asked of me a letter of love and I write to you on that subject. It shines with delight from eyes like yours and its light will doubtless come back a thousand times to illumine your own life. There is no love I or anyone can give that will be of greater help and hope than the love you yourself possess. Its going out will be its return. Trust in the love you have and it will not be misplaced.

Yours
John Clare

It was hardly inspiring stuff and I told Mrs Emmerson so. She informed me that Miss Richardson, a governess at General Reynardson's, had accosted Mr Clare in the garden of the house one afternoon and asked him, on hearing he was a poet, to write her love letters. This document was the response to her rather pert request.

As the story was explained, Mr Clare arrived and I recognised him at once as the man I had met in my own home. The verses he read were in some cases merely adequate, but in others they were more stimulating, and the possibilities touched upon in Miss Richardson's request raised an interest in me that might otherwise never have been excited. On my return home I enquired of my husband and he told me of the circumstances of Mr Clare's visit and his petition for a post in our home.

I went again the following week to hear Mr Clare read in Mrs Emmerson's home. On closer observation I could see why Miss Richardson had framed her request to the scribbler. He was not unappealing. He was a short man, without the immediate physical attraction of some of his fellows, but there was that mixture of raw intelligence and the earthiness of one who, otherwise, might never have entered our drawing rooms.

I determined to find more out for myself and one evening I sent word that I should expect Mr Clare at my home the following morning. Not wanting to appear overly eager, I asked that he bring a selection of his verses for my scrutiny.

He did not come. I spent the morning watching the rain-swept avenue for his approach. In the afternoon, as the rain closed into darkness, I reread the letter he had written to Miss Richardson. (I had inadvertently forgotten to return it to Mrs Emmerson.) I began to detect something less than kindness in it, and the evening brought with it a certainty that the letter was one of coldness. And now he had the nerve to ignore my invitation! I could not suffer such ingratitude lightly.

The following morning's sunlight did little to dispel my humour and then suddenly, there he was, in the garden outside. When, finally, I bade him enter, he was full of apologies for his absence on the previous day. He beat so much about the bush that in the end I asked him to give an account, clearly and promptly, as to why he had not come.

'The rain,' he mumbled.

'It was raining rain, Mr Clare, not fire and brimstone,' I said.

He blushed and mumbled again.

'Kindly explain yourself,' I repeated.

'My boots would not keep out the rain,' he said quickly, keeping his eyes upon the ground, 'and I did not dare to come into your house with stockings that were wringing wet.'

For a moment I thought he was being clever but then

I realised the truth of the situation. I had but to look at his feet to see the veracity of his claim.

'I would have sent one of the children to inform you but . . .' He left the statement incomplete. There were all the children, he explained, and his wife Martha and himself and his only income at that time was writing.

But I had not brought him into my home to listen to the troubles of his life. 'You must not let this state of affairs come between you and your ambition,' I told him. 'If you become overly concerned with the circumstance of your condition today, you will never raise yourself to a better condition tomorrow.'

He seemed to see the sense in that and his manner became more relaxed. We sat and talked about the genesis of his interest in writing and then I asked him to read me some verses.

'Read me the first piece that comes to hand,' I said.

He picked a sheet from the pile by his side and read for me, glancing from the page to my face and back at intervals. When he had concluded I took the page from his hand and read it for myself.

I sleep with thee and wake with thee,
And yet thou art not there:—
I fill my arms, with thoughts of thee,
And press the common air, —
Thy eyes are gazing upon mine,
When thou art out of sight;

My lips are always touching thine,
At morning, noon and night.

I finished reading the lines and observed the man seated opposite. He was staring at me. I felt myself a little uneasy and yet a little startled, aroused even. It was not the man and it was not the verse, which had been written for someone else, or perhaps simply as an exercise in rhyme, but it was the combination of the two – words and man – which was so disconcerting. There was a certain naïve sweetness in the words but there was a deeper, darker side to this man. And he struck me as one who might supply the intrigue and stimulation then absent from my life – the excitement of a flirtation and perhaps something bolder. And I determined to delve more thoroughly into his mind.

I saw no merit in waiting until another time and another opportunity occurred. If one has a question then one must put that question. 'Tell me, Mr Clare,' I said, 'when you and Mrs Clare were courting, where did you do your courting?'

He was quite open and unabashed in his reply. 'Everywhere,' he said.

I pressed onward. 'And your lovemaking? Was that done everywhere too?' I asked.

He blushed at this, to my surprise, and yet I felt he would, with encouragement, open himself to me.

'Oh come now,' I said, 'you cannot be bashful with

me. We are friends, are we not? It is my intention to help you in whatever ways I may. We shall be accomplices in your poetic plans, shall we not?'

He nodded at this but did not speak.

'Today has been, perhaps, less well judged than it might have been. It comes in the shadow of yesterday's disappointment,' I told him. 'Let us begin again next week. You shall come here on Tuesday and we shall walk in the garden and discuss your verse and then we shall decide on what may be best done to enhance your career.'

He stood and mumbled something and bowed.

'You might, perhaps, leave me a selection of your verse so that I may prepare myself to discuss the stronger points and the shortcomings with you,' I added. 'I shall choose a dozen verses at random.'

'I'll happily leave them all to your ladyship,' he said.

'No,' I replied, 'a dozen will suffice.' I did not want to face his expectation of my commenting on every rhyme he had penned.

I counted out the twelve, we set a time for his return on the following Tuesday and our first private audience concluded.

I read his verses that evening. They were ordinary in the extreme, promising in places, but no more than that. I made notes of my suggested alterations. (I did not want him to feel that my interest was simply in him.) Indeed, in a number of instances I fancied the results of my corrections to be quite successful. My improvements in the grammatical constructions made the pieces immediately more pleasant to eye and ear. A number of the verses jarred because of the colloquial nature of the language. This was something I had expected in conversation but had not been prepared for in the written form. Certainly, at the readings in Mrs Emmerson's home there had been none of these expressions. They were distractions and I made notes suggesting new words, or in some instances lines, which would more adequately capture the imagination of the audience which he hoped to attract.

I put a great deal of effort into my reconstruction of his work. But as I remarked earlier, kindness is often ill received by those on whom it is bestowed. But that was still a time away.

On the following Tuesday Mr Clare did arrive at the appointed time and we walked in the garden and I read over the verses in their corrected form and explained the changes to him. In some cases he accepted what I said but in others he was quite adamant that no changes were necessary and that he wished to retain the local expressions which I had amended. I pointed out that he might wish this for his friends and neighbours but a book-buying public in London would not be impressed by such obscurity. In the end he agreed to review his verses and consider my proposals.

'I wish to take you with me to recite for friends of mine,' I told him. 'And they will be appreciative, you know that. Guineas, subscriptions, donations, contributions, books. Guineas. In order to benefit one must conform. And one must listen to one's friends. And we must be friends, must we not?'

He nodded. 'Aye,' he said.

'Come with me,' I said and I led him into the house and up the stairs and into my private sitting room.

'There,' I said, 'do you see this fine writing desk and this chair and these inks and quills and papers?'

He nodded and mumbled.

'I am giving you these to help with your writing,' I told him.

He seemed genuinely grateful for the assistance. More grateful than for any introductions or visits I had suggested to him.

He was taciturn when it came to the question of human contact. I blame that on his peasant background. He could, indeed, deal with things – with desks and chairs and paper and poems – but he could not deal with people of another class. Doubtless he was quite successful with women of his own class. I have heard so many stories of his escapades and from so many sources that they cannot all be concoctions of idle minds. But how many times did I take him to talk in company and found him inebriate beyond description within the hour, having consumed as much wine as quickly as possible? I suspect his manner of lovemaking may have been of a similar short, sharp nature. Or so it seems safe to assume. Certainly, in the matter of drink, he was incapable of controlling his intake or the effects it had on his behaviour. He became, by turns, loud and offensive or dull and forbidding and neither state was particularly pleasant to deal with. On the first occasion I put the matter down to his nervousness but its repetition made me aware of his inability to deal with society beyond his own upbringing. At his worst he resembled a wild animal in an enclosed space, unpredictable, dangerous and a threat to all within his reach.

His tongue, too, would loosen foolishly, becoming either political or coarse and tasteless. Which may have been acceptable in the alehouses where he seemed to think he had an audience but was certainly unacceptable in the houses into which I took him.

His greatest folly of all was the assumption that his own class should be impressed by him. But he was one of their own who had stepped, even temporarily, out of the pit and was no sooner cleaned up and polished than they began the none too difficult task of dragging him back among them. He was more than capable of slipping back himself. They were jealous of his day in the light, and raised to a state of ecstasy by his fall. Not one of them was sufficiently interested in his welfare to make the journey to see him in the madhouse. Not even his wife!

However, to return to the development of our relationship. I was at pains to ensure that he saw me as a friend of his. My gift had been an attempt to remove whatever barriers his lowly station might create for us. I was truly interested in his welfare. I wanted success for him and I wanted to fortify the bond between us. I was making myself available and putting my position at some risk in doing so and in return I sought some commitment from Mr Clare.

After I had made my gift known and after he had examined the desk and papers I took him back into the garden and we walked together again and I put my initial question to him.

'Will you write verses for me, John?' I asked. 'Will you write love letters, just for me?'

'If you wish,' he said.

'I do wish,' I said.

He nodded his assent.

'And would you wish for anything?' I asked.

He seemed to spend a long time thinking upon this and finally he stopped his walking and turned to me and said, very quietly but with great tenderness, it seemed: 'Perhaps a likeness of your ladyship.'

Such had been the length of the request in coming that I found it almost a disappointment and yet he was requesting something of a personal nature and I agreed at once, promising a locket and likeness within the week.

'You shall have it,' I said. 'And I shall have my love letters.'

That moment promised much, I thought. And one afternoon, perhaps a month afterwards, we drove in my carriage to Mrs Holden's home, where Mr Clare was to read for some ladies who were interested in his progress. In the course of the journey he was more open than hitherto. He told me about his childhood pastimes, the games he played, the music he learned on his violin, the first rude verses he had composed and how he would read them for his father and pretend they were penny ballads he had learned from a passing singer. And he told me of his dancing days. He described to me dances I had never seen performed. He sang me songs that he had collected. He was, altogether, a different man.

When we arrived at Mrs Holden's home he read his verse and spoke with the ladies and then I asked him to show us the dances he had spoken of on our journey. I asked Mrs Holden to send for one of the gardener's boys and have him bring in two sticks from the yard. Then we settled to watch Mr Clare demonstrate his dancing steps with the boy.

He seemed most wary of my request and was slow in making any move to illustrate the dances he had spoken of, so that I began to wonder whether they existed anywhere but in his imagination. I suggested this to him and at once he began to move, not gracefully, but rapidly through a series of passes, clapping his stick against the boy's stick and twirling as he moved, thumping his foot on the floor and at all times fixing the boy with his eyes. And each time their sticks clashed he brought his down with greater force until at length his stick smashed the other and he came to a stop. The boy was holding his hand and blood was flowing from a wound above the knuckles.

Mrs Holden clapped her hands and signalled to the boy that he might go. He left the room and, immediately, Mr Clare followed him and I heard him speaking with the boy in the hallway.

As we drove home he chided me for insisting that he dance. 'I hurt that boy and that should not have happened,' he said.

'I merely requested a demonstration,' I replied. 'Nothing more.'

'You should not have done. You made me angry. I should not have struck him, even without intention.'

I laughed at this and pointed out that my asking him to dance was hardly justification or excuse for his having wounded the boy.

'You should not have put us in that position, him or me,' he said.

And to make matters worse, I discovered later, through a conversation with Mrs Holden, that he had given the boy a crown for his troubles — and this from a man who could barely feed his children. As if the boy had never been wounded before and as if all of this led back in some inexplicable way to my little request.

The simple explanation for this incident and for his frequent drunkenness lies in his inability to cope with the things to which he aspired. Aspiration is not enough if one does not possess the gift of acceptance. Mr Clare was forever looking backward and forward and as a result was unable to keep his feet steady or his head clear at times when that was demanded by the company to which he had been introduced. The problem was as easy and as complex as that.

Aware as I was of my own desires, I was also aware of the necessity for keeping appearances and to this end I made a point of visiting his cottage on a number of occasions, to talk with Mrs Clare and the children. I cannot deny being surprised by the cleanliness and warmth of the Clares' cottage. The children were well nourished, well washed and well behaved. The house itself was nothing if not clean. It was a large cottage by the standards of Mr Clare's class, being possessed of three bedrooms, a sitting room, a kitchen and a back kitchen.

It had been made, at Mr Clare's request, with the door to the back, so that he could step straight into his garden.

He was greatly proud of this garden, not for its neatness but rather for the wildness he had cultivated in it. Rarely have I seen him more animated than the first time he walked me through it. He was thoroughly enraptured by it. He had transplanted many flowers from their native grounds, taking them with clumps of their soil, and put them into his own. Many I should have passed off as weeds but these were among the plants he was most enamoured of: horehound, oxlip, basil, bugloss, mullein, were all pointed out to me. I offered him some of the plants from my own garden but these, he said, 'would hardly sit in such a wilderness as this'.

I mentioned his inability to hold his drink to Mrs Clare and she seemed to share my dislike for it.

'But,' she added, 'he cannot be easy in an alehouse unless he is well drunk, he fears the scorn of his neighbours unless he is as drunk as they.'

That hardly seemed an adequate explanation for his behaviour in other company but I saw little point in pursuing this matter with her. It would be of little import to her and would make no difference to him.

As the weather, that first summer of our acquaintance, grew more warming so his moods seemed greatly to improve and his companionship became more pleasant. My husband spent much of that summer in London and I determined to have Mr Clare for myself.

One afternoon in that July he and I were seated in my

sitting room. The windows were thrown open and the
sun was heating the soft breeze that carried the scent of
the garden to the deepest corners of my home. It was an
altogether idyllic afternoon. Mr Clare had read me some
of his verse and I had made my reactions known to him
and he had not dismissed them. We were speaking of the
experiences of childhood. I told him of mine and he told
me of his.

He described his perpetual search, as a child, for the
land rail – a little-seen bird – among the summer wheat.
He recollected evenings when he and his sister would
attempt to race the moon on their way back home,
flying like clouds in its face and never succeeding in
reaching home before it. He laughed a great, deep laugh
when he spoke of that. The most sincere laughter I ever
heard him take.

Gently, I moved the conversation on to later times
and I enquired, finally, of his courtship and whether it
had been of only one woman.

He replied that it had not.

'Of many?' I asked.

'Some,' he said.

I feared he was about to become sullen and withdrawn
again but I ventured onward with my questioning. 'Was
there one you loved especially?'

He was silent but it was not a sullen silence now,
instead he seemed deeply moved.

'I may take it that there was,' I continued.

He nodded.

I recall leaning forward in my chair and reaching across and putting my hands on his and then, very softly, kneeling before him, my face looking up into his, divided between the desire to kiss and the need to know what story might be there to be told, a story never heard, perhaps, by another soul.

'Tell me,' I whispered, 'tell me some intimacy of your courtship. In one courtship. Tell me something you have never told anyone else in your life.'

He was silent for a very long time and I feared he might not respond to me.

'Please,' I whispered, even more quietly than before.

He began to speak so slowly that it was difficult at first to decide whether there was any connection between the words he was uttering. But gradually the sense of what he was saying began to emerge.

'I were in . . . I love . . . once, always, with a girl as I met in school.'

I continued staring into his face, into his eyes. Our eyes were staring each into the other's and yet I think he saw nothing of me.

'Tell me her name, tell me this girl's name,' I whispered.

'Mary Joyce.'

He paused again and I moved my hand from where

it rested on his, along the sleeve of his shirt and up onto his shoulder and then my fingers touched the strands of his wild hair. I stroked them as though they were the most delicate petals on a prized rose, so softly that he would hardly have sensed my fingers brushing him. And then he began to speak and I went on touching his hair. He spoke quietly but with great sureness, intent on telling his story.

'I were writing poems for her,' he said, 'but I never felt free to tell her this and I would never dare give them to her. All that time I were writing for her . . . to her . . . and I were afraid to let her see the words I had wrote for her. I could not find the way to tell her and I could never muster the courage to tell her my feelings for her.'

He stopped speaking and I pressed the palm of my hand against the side of his face. His eyes were still unwavering in their gaze and yet he was not seeing me. If he was aware of a presence at all, it was not of mine. And then he returned to his story in that same low, set voice.

'One Sunday evening,' he continued, 'when I knew she was at church, I took a book of love poems as I'd bought for myself and I put flowers in two of the pages, forget-me-nots, and I stood outside the church until people started to leave. It were raining and it were evening, but a warm evening, and she come out with her father. He went away to get their cart and she stood in the shelter of the church doorway and I come out of the shelter I were standing in and I handed her the book, I reached out and put it into her hand.'

His eyes seemed to take on a light, a life, as though he were either seeing me for the first time or he was seeing through me, past me. I remained kneeling and then he went on talking, as though he had never paused at all.

'She never looked at the book, not a glance. She looked at me and spoke not a word and neither did I. We stood there in the rain without speaking a single word between us. And then her father called to her that the cart were ready and she went away.'

I said nothing for some time, thinking there might be more to be told, but at length it was obvious that he had no more to say.

'Did you make love to her? Later?' I asked.

He shook his head.

'I should like to make love to you, John,' I said and I took his hand in mine and pressed it to my face. 'I gave you my likeness. You asked it of me. You found it attractive. Do you find me attractive, John?'

'Aye,' he said.

'Come with me, then, where we shall not be disturbed.'

I led him up to my bedroom. There, too, the windows were thrown wide on the glorious afternoon. I pulled the curtains closed and turned to face him. He was standing, so uneasy, in the centre of the room. I moved towards him and stood, my breasts against his shirt, looking up into his eyes, waiting for him to touch me.

He shook his head several times. At first I thought it was a sign of admiration, but then he spoke.

'I cannot do it,' he said.

'Surely it isn't that you are afraid?' I said.

He said nothing.

'It can hardly be that you have not made love to another woman since your marriage?'

'No,' he said, 'it isn't that. I cannot do it. I cannot be at ease here.'

'Let us go elsewhere, then,' I said.

'It isn't that neither,' he said. 'I do find you attractive but it would not be right with me, I could not be at ease and so it would not be good . . . for you.'

'May I not be the judge of that?' I said.

He went on shaking his head and I knew nothing would come of this. I felt anger, not shame but something like it. The sting of his rejection resembled that of a thistle on the skin. The discourtesy and arrogance of this saucebox was as demeaning as it was unwarranted.

'Wait for me downstairs,' I told him.

And I left him waiting for a long time.

When I went down to my sitting room I took with me a violin that had lain about the house for many years, unused. I handed it to Mr Clare.

'Will you, at least, play for me?' I asked.

He took the violin and began to tune it. I poured myself a glass of wine.

'What shall you play for me?' I asked. 'I should like to know what I am about to hear.'

' "Nancy Dawson",' he said.

'Is this one of your own collecting?' I said.

'No,' he replied.

'Very well,' I said, walking to the window. 'Play for me.'

Something in my tone must have surprised and frightened him for his eyes narrowed and his face was suddenly pipe white.

'Play me the tune,' I repeated.

He began to play and as he did I walked about the room until I came towards him face to face, and in an instant I splashed my glass of wine across his face. The red wine dripped from his hair and face onto his white linen shirt. I stayed but long enough to take the scene in and then I swept from the room and left him to find his own way out and home.

I did not see Mr Clare again that month and was not sure I should ever see him, other than by chance. But he did reappear, unannounced, and spent much time in apology for his behaviour. It crossed my mind that he had come, perhaps, at a time when he was hopeful of the completion of my suggested intimacy but if this was so then he was greatly disappointed for I never mentioned it to him.

I did, however, tell him that I had been appraised, by Mrs Emmerson, of the fact that he had submitted a poem to his publisher which contained lines about 'accursed wealth o'erbounding human laws'. I asked him whether this was true and he replied that it was so.

'He has insisted on the poem's removal,' I told him. 'You know you cannot publish that kind of sedition. You know that.'

He said nothing.

'And you have written verses attacking the hunt,' I went on.

'Aye,' he muttered, 'and badger-baiting.'

This I could not accept, not after what had gone before, and certainly not in my own home.

'I know nothing of that,' I said. 'That is among your own people. But the hunt is part of England, part of its history.'

'A bloody, brutal part,' he said.

Suddenly his boldness was growing. I turned on him in a fury.

'A part,' I reiterated. 'You cannot hope for continued support if you insist on writing this kind of seditious nonsense. You are someone now, you are a writer, a poet, a person of standing who has access to the homes of the highest. Have I not taken you into houses myself, have I not introduced you to influential people, people who will be of assistance to you, people who will open ways that would never have been open to you? Have you not met important people in London because of your position?'

There was no retort. I took the opportunity to drive the point to its conclusion.

'You must see the senselessness, the treason, the danger to your standing and to your family in all of this. You must stick to the things you know of, the rhymes of rivers and fields and birds.'

'I have never wrote of fields,' he interrupted.

'Don't talk to me of enclosure,' I sighed. 'I do not want to hear of it. It is done. Done. You must accept the things that are done, John. Just as you must accept the responsibilities that go with your position. You owe it to those of us who have facilitated your position.'

Again, he was silent.

'And you have not used your writing desk,' I said.

'I am waiting to take it home,' he said.

And I believe he meant it.

'Home! Home!' I said when I had recovered. And then I laughed. 'Surely you did not think it was for taking home? No, it is there for your use, as you require it, in my home. That is why I made it available. So that you could come and write in my home. Where you could have peace. Quietness. Where you and I could be close. Where I could be on hand to advise you on the finer points of your work.'

He seemed genuinely deflated.

'And when did you last write me a love letter?' I asked. 'When did you last speak with me? More than a month ago. No love letters. Nothing.'

I stood again, as I had stood a month earlier, my body close to his.

'Undo your britches for me,' I said.

He hesitated. There were so many emotions in that hesitation, not least the awakening of desire and possibility. That thrilled me, it restored my self-belief. But there were other emotions too. Fear, loathing, embarrassment, uncertainty.

'Undo your britches,' I repeated.

Slowly he undid them and when he had done I took his hands in mine and held them momentarily, long enough for his britches to slide about his ankles. There he stood, as I had done, like a fool. I saw the pathetic comedy in the figure before me and I laughed and laughed and laughed. The moment was mine.

I do not accept the claim that my encounter with Mr Clare contributed in any way to the decline in his ability to reason and to live a life that might be described as normal. There was a battle raging within his own head and it was not bettered or worsened by anything I or anyone else did for or against him.

I date Mr Clare's deterioration from the failure of his verse to sell. Initially, there had been a fascination with this strange man and his writings. But many of those who would question my involvement with Mr Clare would already have deserted him once he ceased to be a passing fancy. I at least remained involved. He could not, however, cope with the fact that he was not destined for a central place on the London literary stage. His fame there was fleet. And in his own area his fame was nothing. He was a laughing stock. Once the dual nature of his rejection became clear the sinister collapse of his brain was hastened. That is my analysis and I was well placed to observe it.

Only once did I see his mental state at its most violent. That was one afternoon in autumn when I called unannounced at his cottage. I rounded the corner into the garden, by way of entering the cottage, and was confronted by the sight, through the open door, of Mr Clare smashing his fists and face against the kitchen table while at the same time screaming incomprehensibly. His wife ran past me to the end of their garden and called to their daughter, who came hurriedly from the field beyond and rushed inside.

A moment later all was quiet and then she led Mr Clare out through the doorway, still muttering and cursing, and bleeding from a gash above the bridge of his nose, but calmer than he had been. She led him as you would lead an infant, down the garden path and into the pasture beyond and out across the fens. Mrs Clare explained that this was the only cure for his anger and that their daughter Eliza was the only one with whom he would walk.

'He may walk with her for hours now,' she told me, 'but he will come back quieter and we will have at least seven or eight days of peace afore this happens again.'

I cannot deny that I thought of the afternoons in my own home, only a couple of years earlier – I even knelt before this same man – and I shivered at the thought of what might have been.

I was not surprised when I heard that he had been incarcerated in an asylum for the deranged. I was, however, taken aback that he had been admitted to High Beach, an asylum in the Epping forest. The sanity of the man who ran that establishment was, in itself, suspect. Had he not maintained that one part of society was at war with another and that this was one of the reasons for the existence of insanity! It seemed as though he had been reading, and heeding, the rantings of Mr Clare himself. Fate had matched doctor and patient, it seemed to me.

His internment brought many sympathisers. They claimed, among other things, that his state was not one of insanity or delirium but rather of anxiety brought on by poverty and bodily exhaustion. When I heard opinions such as these I was tempted to mention his incessant inebriation, his incessant wenching and his incessant turn of ill-chosen and offensive poetic statements. But I did not. Soon enough these people would find that the hand that feeds is often bitten.

I was, however, astounded to hear of Mr Clare's return to his home. He had been absent for three years and the reports we had received had not suggested the possibility of return. Indeed, we had settled into the expectation of his long-term incarceration and then suddenly, there was word that he was home again.

It was July when he returned but our paths did not cross until late in that August when, one radiant evening, he appeared on my lawn. I saw him and thought it best to face him down. But he was quite removed from any state of anxiety and smiled when I approached. My own fears were somewhat allayed by the sight of his daughter loitering at the further end of the lawn. Evidently she had been sent to be his guardian angel in his wanderings.

'I'm pleased to see you back among us, John,' I said.

'I'm pleased to be back,' he said.

'Is your writing going well?' I asked.

'Well indeed,' he said.

He wandered away from me and began to smell, deeply, the roses that provided a shelter along the pathway.

'If you wish to take some flowers with you, for Mrs Clare, please do,' I said.

'No, we have flowers enough in our own garden,' he said. 'Not roses such as these but all kinds of flowers. I have spent the day watching the silver-washed butterflies among them.'

'You have settled back then?' I asked.

'Well settled. And free,' he replied.

'I'm glad to hear that,' I said. 'We shall look forward to hearing you read for us all again in the autumn. You must have a great deal of new verse to choose from.'

'A great deal,' he said.

We walked on, he asking me the names of roses, I asking about the direction his verse was taking. It was a perfectly amicable hour we spent together and it was he who first made his excuses and left.

I was happy for him, for though I still harboured then, and still do now, the bitter memory of an earlier time, I never wished him the awful sickness that had struck him so terribly.

We did not meet again until December and then it was in Stamford one afternoon, when we came face to face in the street. He was carrying a sheaf of papers and again his daughter was following at a distance.

'I see you have been writing,' I said, referring to the papers under his arm.

'I have,' he said.

I was about to make some other remark when he continued: 'Would you like me to read you a new verse?'

'Very much,' I said. 'We must arrange a reading where we can hear a selection.'

'I shall read you one now,' he said.

I assumed it was something freshly written, something of great pride. 'Of course,' I assented.

And then he knelt in the street, and began as if to read from one of the sheets that he carried.

'Our father, which art in heaven . . .' he said.

I thought for an instant that this was an introduction but the lunacy of his kneeling in the public thoroughfare and the words which followed made it clear that it was not.

'. . . hallowed be thy name,' he continued. 'Thy kingdom come, thy will be done on earth as it is in heaven. Give us this day our daily bread, forgive us our trespasses, as we forgive them that trespass against us and lead us not into temptation but deliver us from evil, for Thine is the kingdom, the power and the glory, for ever and ever. Amen.'

I had stood among the gaping throng while this went on and now I signalled to his daughter to come and take him away. She came and stood by him and waited until he had got to his feet again. So calm was she that the possibility fleetingly crossed my mind that this performance was his way of publicly humiliating me but then he turned his attention from me and began to search the faces of passing girls, at the same time shouting loudly as he went. The words were a mockery of those he had already spoken. I could not but hear them, for his voice rose above the clamour of the street.

'Mary Joyce, who were in my heart,' he shouted, 'blessed be thy name. Thy loving come, thy will be done in this place as it was in that time. Give me this day thy needed love and forgive me my absence, as I forgive thee thine, and lead me into temptation, deliver me from loneliness, for thine are the eyes, the lips, the breasts, for ever and ever. Amen.'

I was transfixed by this display of madness. The women to whom he addressed his tirade were either terrified or amused. Some laughed, some ran from his effrontery. His daughter merely allowed the harangue to come to its natural conclusion. It seemed, momentarily, that it had, when suddenly Clare threw himself into the roadway and began a series of shrieks that made me weak. These sounds stopped briefly and then recommenced, but as distinguishable words.

'Sweet Jesus, Mary Joyce,' he screamed over and over again until his voice grew hoarse.

Finally, some men of the town succeeded in quieting him and they led him away, past the spot where I stood. He was muttering the opening words of the Lord's

Prayer over and over to himself as he went.

I returned to my carriage and travelled homeward, shocked and trembling at what I had seen.

Now I can recall the anticipation, the disappointment, the ennui in trying to deal with a man whose expectations were so narrow, a man who claimed that the enclosure would curb freedom and imagination and yet a man who, even in his sanest moments, was incapable of anything other than profanity.

It is sad, pathetic, to see any human fall to these depths but particularly one whose talents were clear, if limited. One would not wish such a curse on any human being. A struggle regarding the hurt of the heart is one thing, a plague of the mind is another. But this plague, this disease, is nothing to do with the inadequacies which led to my suffering at the hands of Mr Clare. Nothing. He was, then, a different man. I feel pity for the creature he became but I feel rage and loathing for the man he was. I make no connection between the two.

IV

Eliza Clare

MY FATHER SPENT the last two dozen years of his life in the asylum for the mad, St Andrew's in Northampton. When I say that, it may sound clean and easy but it was not so. All of us — wife, children, family — were affected by my father's illness. And having him removed from the family was not a simple way of dealing with the problem. Just as the removal of a damaged arm or leg from the body cannot be said to be the end of the damage. The limb remains in the mind and the regret at its loss continues for as long as there is life in the body. We did not breathe a sigh of relief when my father was taken away a second and final time to the asylum. We lived in hope that he might return at some period to live with us. Our hope was that he might become better, or at least passive, and be capable of staying with us and doing the things he was happiest in doing – writing, tending to his flowers, walking on the fens, talking with his neighbours, observing the changes in the natural world. These are elementary things and are not beyond the capabilities of most people. To know that is to know the closeness of the possibility of having my father return. And as regret remains, so hope remains and each day brings the chance of return.

We would visit my father in Northampton whenever we could but it was difficult. The four pounds for the journey was not readily come by. As we grew older it became easier but when my father was first taken into High Beach asylum, in Essex, I was but a girl of fifteen and when he was finally taken from us I was nineteen and only finding my own way in the world. It is not my place to say but I was, of all his children, the one who seemed most to be in his company. I saw him, in childhood, as a man who knew all that was worth knowing in the way of nature. And he shared this knowledge with all of us.

My Aunt Sophy often remarked that I was as close to

him in my childhood as she had been in hers, and so it seems I was, for I cannot recall anything in my youngest days that did not have my father's presence. No journey, no matter how brief, no occasion was complete without his figure in the landscape of my memory. His arms seemed eternally to be about me – holding me, hugging me, swinging me, throwing me into the air and catching me. But as I grew my father seemed gradually to change and the man I knew became, in ways, a stranger. His reactions were less predictable. His depressions were of greater duration. His laughter and happiness seemed uncustomary. I could not then assess the changes that were taking place but I was caught in situations which I realised, even as a young girl, were not natural. Among my friends I knew of no other father who spent as much time with his children as my father did but neither did I know of any father who could seem so removed from the world about him.

No other father would rant in the street against badger-baiting; no other father would fall to his knees in prayer in the market place and then seem not to recall what he had done. And no other daughter seemed constantly charged with the responsibility of watching for these strangenesses. Not that I objected. It merely required my being with my father, or in a position to observe him, much of the time. And this was the case, anyway. He rarely went about his ramblings without one or more of us, and I seemed the one most often chosen. Not that I was oldest or youngest but that I seemed most interested in all he wrote and said.

I set this before you not to claim a special closeness, for I was unaware of it, but because this is how things transpired in our lives. I think his love for reading was most thoroughly observed and copied in my life. I am grateful for that gift, though I am grateful, too, that it did not impinge upon my acquaintance with normality. My father paid that extortionate price in his own life and lived to regret it. I saw that with my own eyes and heard it from his lips on many an occasion.

But I was not the only one affected by the events of his illness. All of us were dealt blows of our own. My mother was left without a husband at a time when she should have been in the prime of her enjoyment of companionship. When he was taken to High Beach she lived in hope that he would recover. His incarceration there was offered as a hopeful thing. He would return as the man she had married. Even his letters to her spoke of this. She never made the journey to see him there, nor did any of us. It was beyond our means. And she was sick with the palsy much of the time. Another burden sent for her to bear. But she did see my father again. For some months. That was in the summer and through to the year's end of eighteen hundred and forty-one.

My father had, at that time, been three years in the

asylum in the Epping forest and we had had letters and calls from a great many people who had been to visit him there. All of them spoke of his comfort and his good temper. His letters came too, and I would read them to my mother. Some of them seemed to augur well; they were full of hope and talk of home. But others were confused and painful. Even in my eighteenth year I began to keep the true contents of some of these letters from my mother. I would read only those passages which seemed appropriate to her capacity to accept the sadness they delivered. Not that I kept his illness from her, merely that I did not always tell her of the references his letters contained to other women. Some of these were known to me and to my mother. Others seemed to be women he had met at High Beach. And still others, I believe, were creatures of his imagination.

One name recurred with terrible regularity. That of Mary Joyce. I was aware from my mother's conversations of her existence in my father's growing years and of her death. Indeed, I had gone once to see her grave. It was in the wake of a series of letters my father had sent, addressed to her. I went to satisfy myself that she was dead. I derived some peace of mind from the sight of her name carved into the stone. I dropped a spray of blooms onto the grave, not from any sense of sorrow, but rather from one of gratitude.

However, to return to my father's reappearance. It

was in the month of July of eighteen hundred and forty-one. His life in High Beach had been one of relative freedom. His master, Dr Allen, had allowed him to come and go as he pleased, with only the eyes of his keepers cast irregularly upon him. This was part of Dr Allen's method of encouraging a responsibility which might lead to a return to full health. My father took advantage of this freedom to make the acquaintance of a large number of people – householders, gypsies, children, inmates, shopkeepers – as well as those writers and patrons who called to visit him.

In a letter sent to us at the Easter of that year he wrote of a visit to Buckhurst church on Easter day and of seeing a child there who reminded him of my brother William. 'A small boy with a serious face', he wrote. Afterwards I saw in that short, sad reference a spur which gave him the reason for wanting to get back to his home and his family.

That freedom had allowed him to make his hasty plans and execute them. He was well clear of High Beach before his absence was reported. And he had the sense to avoid detection, despite lookouts along his journey. In three days he walked the eighty miles from High Beach to our home but he was ill-prepared for the rigours of the journey, taking no food or money in his pocket, intent only on getting back to his home and his family.

He slept, as he had done in his youth, my mother said, in fields and ditches upon the way. He told me afterwards that he slept the first night with his first wife – in that he meant Mary Joyce – upon his left side. When he awoke the next morning she was not there, he said.

'Someone came and took her away from my side,' he told me. 'I searched about the field I were sleeping in and the next field and along the roadway, thinking she might have gone walking without me, but I never discovered her and knew that she would not have left me by her own choosing. Someone came and took her away from me.'

It made me sad to hear him talk of his first wife and sad to hear him say he was alone on waking. I think he was alone for most of his life. He had his family in his own childhood and us in his manhood but he was always alone.

On the second night of his escape he slept in the porch of a doorway. Though it was July, the night was cool and he told me how he gazed through a window of this house and was mesmerised by the glowing of a fire in the grate. He imagined it to be a house he could have lived in with his first wife, he said. But he was afraid to knock and ask for lodging, fearing he would be taken back to High Beach.

Each time he spoke to me of his first wife it cut me for myself and for our family and most for our mother.

Because she could neither read nor write there are those who make the assumption that she could not feel the pain of always being second to this other woman, this ghost who could do no wrong because she was safe within the grave. It is my mother who could do little in the way of wrong. She accepted all that my father delivered in the way of loyalty and betrayal. Some of that betrayal came from the sickness in his mind but much of it came from his continual dissatisfaction with his life and that was something my mother was not the cause of. Rather, she did all in her power to make life pleasant for him and us.

I loved my father dearly. I was closer to him than any of his other children but I see, too, the infidelity, the difficulty of living with him as my mother did. One moment she was the object of great affection and gentleness and the next she was his second wife, or worse, she was left while he pursued some other woman who had caught his eye.

The other thing my father told me about those nights spent in the open was that he always slept with his head in the direction he must walk the following day. He was in search of a ghost and taken up with the fantasies of a sick mind and yet he had the wit to sleep with his head in the direction of our home. That, too, is a sadness. So much sickness and yet so much that is clever. So much possibility and so little hope.

On his third day of walking, he told me, he was so hungry that he ate grass from the roadside. He assured me 'it tasted as good as bread'. He told me how he considered his position then.

'There I was, a man whose daughter is the queen of England, seated on a heap of stones, without a farthing to my name. And yet, I thought, if I put fresh speed into my step then I shall see my family tomorrow, and so I walked on.'

A man from Helpston saw him and he six miles from our home and I took a cart and went out to meet him. He was seated on a stile, three miles from Northborough, when first I saw him. He looked a melancholy sight, his face dirty, his shoes torn, his shirt stained. And yet I was more happy than I could say to see him. Had he not escaped, made his way as true as a stone to the home where his family lived? Had he not been valiant in his efforts to be reunited with us?

I alighted from the cart and walked towards him. He looked at me as he might have looked on any stranger passing the way.

'You know me, Father?' I asked.

He shook his head.

'I am Eliza, your daughter.'

Still his stare was blank.

'You have walked a great way. We were told you were walking and I came to meet you.'

He smiled at this.

'My mother is waiting for you at home. I have brought Morgan's cart so that you may travel the last miles in comfort.'

'You would take me back to the madhouse,' he said.

'No, Father,' I assured him. 'I will take you home.'

He smiled again at this. 'You have devised this to take me to the madhouse,' he said, shaking his head.

'Father, if I were to take you to the madhouse, should I have come out here alone, without strong men to take you with them. I shall bring you home. To your wife.'

He seemed puzzled by this and sat a long time without speaking. I sat by him on the stile. Finally, he seemed to have reached an understanding of what I had said.

'Patty?' he asked.

'Yes, Father, your wife Patty,' I said.

'You will take me to her?' he asked.

'Yes,' I said, as gently as I could.

I took his arm and we walked to the cart and he looked inside several times before he had satisfied himself that this was not a way of capturing him.

'Where is my other wife?' he asked then.

'Who be that, Father?' I asked.

He became indignant at once.

'My first wife,' he shouted. 'Mary Joyce.'

'She is dead, Father,' I said, 'this years. I wrote and

told you so.'

'No,' he said quietly, 'I have seen her myself, not two days ago.'

'Perhaps you have,' I said. 'Let us talk about her later. Patty will be waiting for you, and the children.'

He climbed into the cart and we set off for Northborough and our home. My mind was in a muddle. My joy at seeing him had been tempered by the talk of Mary Joyce and by his not knowing me. And yet as we travelled towards home, he seemed to ease back into himself. He chatted with me about the places we passed. He seemed, now, to know exactly who I was and he thanked me for the letters I had sent to him at High Beach.

'The gypsies helped me escape,' he told me. 'They left me a change of clothes and a peeled stick that pointed the way I should walk in order to get here.'

'That's good, Father,' I said.

We were journeying slowly onward and homeward and I was putting my nervousness behind me. It was strange to see so many people come and stand at their doors and watch us making our unhurried way home. And not one of them said other than 'Good morrow, John Clare' or ''Tis good to see you, John.' He smiled at them and searched their faces and I knew he was looking for Mary Joyce, and all the old fear, that had but ten minutes earlier been put from my mind, began to return. But I could not tell him again that she was lying buried this good time, unwed.

And then his mind took to another subject. He looked about him from the cart at all the fields around us – not that they were changed since his last seeing them, but he seemed greatly shocked by the sight.

'They've closed in every pasture,' he said.

'Everything, Father. All in fields,' I said.

'Everything,' he mumbled and then he was silent.

I could only imagine how, in his long days in High Beach, he had dreamed this land of his childhood back to the state it had been in forty years earlier, when he ran freely through unenclosed pastures.

My mother was in tears at the sight of him. She hugged him and held his hand and walked him about the garden a dozen times, telling him how fit and healthy he looked. He smiled at her and we stood back and observed them, as you would young lovers who have been parted.

He commented on how well the garden looked. It was a high summer afternoon and the flowers were showing of their best colours. It was as though we were all back in childhood times with our parents happily looking over the garden. To the observer nothing could seem more perfect and ideal than the sight that we saw. A man and wife, arm in arm in their garden, while inside the cottage their children went about the task of preparing a meal for them. And such was the sight in our home on that July afternoon.

In the following three days my father concerned himself with writing an account of his journey home. In that time, too, Dr Allen sent word that he would be happy to have my father back at High Beach if he or my mother desired this. My mother did not mention this contact to my father. She seemed convinced that he was much better and was anxious to try him at home, hoping that the company of his family would be a further source of recovery.

At home my father was quiet and went about his tasks in the garden with the same enjoyment he had always shown. With the onset of the harvest he appeared in the fields with my brothers. He gave what assistance he could and, indeed, his strength seemed to return as the weeks passed.

One morning he and I set out to follow my brothers to where they were harvesting. We walked through Northborough. The village was deserted.

'It is like winter,' my father said. 'Or like a village frightened of some plundering army.'

I thought his mind was becoming uneasy again but he explained himself more clearly as we walked.

'I have always thought it so,' he said. 'When harvest comes there is not a soul's shadow about the villages, not a child at play, not a mother in a garden, every door is

closed and every window latched. They are all away at
the harvesting. There's a deadness about a village without
children.'

Sometimes he would set off alone across the fens and
one of us would follow at a distance, never allowing him
to know he was being observed. At other times he
would walk to visit someone of his acquaintance and I
would walk with him and wait outside until his
conversation was complete.

On one such day I observed Lady Kettering and my
father walking in her garden. I had met her once when
she called to our home but I had never before seen her
garden. It was full of roses of a thousand shades of red and
yellow and purple. The scent carried down the avenue.
My father told me she had offered him some roses to
take back with him but he had declined.

For the most part, on these journeys, my father's
conversations were of an ordinary nature but there were
times when they took courses that were not predictable.
Sometimes it was simply reminiscence. We would walk
across the edge of the fens on September afternoons and
sit in the sunlight and I would talk or he would talk and
I would listen. Once, he told me very intensely about
how he would sit behind a wall in High Beach and
imagine himself back in Helpston or Northborough
again.

'I would close my eyes and be back here,' he said. 'I

could stop out every sound and be walking here and stop on a woodland stile and hear the pigeons clacking in the oaks.'

On one such afternoon we were talking when suddenly, and with great frustration, he produced a letter from his pocket and handed it to me.

'I have writ this to my first wife and I have nowhere to send it,' he said.

I took the letter and put it in my pocket. In a short time he was calm again and seemed completely to have forgotten it. I kept it, as I kept every word he scribbled or wrote. It seemed that the letter had been written in Northborough and carried about by him in his keeping in the weeks he had been with us. It caused me great pain to read that letter and I was sorely tempted to destroy it but I did not. It read:

My dear wife

I would have told you how I got here but not being able to see you I soon began to feel homeless at home and shall, bye and bye, feel nearly hopeless but not as lonely as I was for here I can see the place we were used to be and know you are safe if not happy. Though my home is no home to me my hopes are not entirely hopeless while even your memory lives so near to me. Believe me as ever I have been and shall be

your affectionate husband

John Clare

Even had he not mentioned for whom this letter was intended, I should have known. It made me feel a dreadful sense of the hopeless. He had, from my reading then and now, accepted Mary Joyce as dead but he had not relinquished the hold she had on him. It seemed the main inspiration for his return to live with us was his intention of being close to the places associated with her. Perhaps I am being overly hard in saying this but it was nothing to the bitterness that rested in my mind for several days thereafter. I could not see my father without wondering what twisted sense was in his head and what thoughts of this dead woman were always swimming there. I did, in time, come to think of that letter as another unplanned piece of scribbling that was forgotten in the hour after it was written and forgotten for ever in the hour after it was given to me. But I have never been quite certain.

There were occasions when his rantings were of a more difficult nature. Occasions when he shouted about the house, shouted at my mother and at me. I recall times when his violence of speech seemed destined to become a violence of act, though it never did.

The worst of these was the first. It was an afternoon in September. We had been quietly about our business when my father came in from the garden where he had been seated in writing. Without a word, he swept what dishes there were from the table. He accused my mother of being 'false' to him.

'I left thee,' he screamed, 'because of thy faults. Untruth is what I left for. Untruth in you. Falseness and untruth. I would never have been away from here were it not for falseness. I was born a poet and you a whore.'

I shouted at him to stop this slander but my mother hushed me.

'Let him have his say, he will be all the quieter,' she said.

'He cannot say the like of that,' I said.

'I can say as I wish,' my father said. 'I was locked away so that she might carry on with other men, sneaking about the place and thinking I did not know. I knew. I heard in people's conversations. It was the talk all over Essex, as far away as that. I should never have married. I was trapped into madness the day I married Patty Turner. When I could, for the asking, have married Betty Sell or Mary Joyce or anyone who was there to be asked.'

I had heard enough at this. There was no reason why my mother should have this thrown in her face after all she had been through and I told my father so. It seemed to stop his onslaught but it was my mother who intervened. She went and got his coat and my cape and asked us to walk together to the fens and settle our differences for she had none with either of us.

And we did walk and it did seem to quiet my father a great deal for he spoke not a word on the outward walk. Returning homeward, he began to talk about the warmth the family gave to his life.

'I could not go out from the cottage if I did not have it to come back to, and it has ever been so,' he said. 'I have always had Patty's love on which to build my life. But I have a fault in that every friendship has grown into a warm attachment and I have believed in all who came to me and put more energy into them that should otherwise, and to better account, have been expended in my own home.'

He left the matter there and so did I. He was not changed, I knew, but he had tried to explain the man he was and that, for then, was as much as might be expected of him.

About this time, too, letters came to our home offering assistance but giving none. They came from my father's acquaintances in London, saying how they had heard of his difficulties and would be happy to assist. He wrote back to all of them immediately.

'I do not wish my hardships to be trumpeted by all and sundry. I have never sought praise or reward and I do

not seek it now. I wish only to live an independent life.
I am not fallen upon charity.'

We might have done with help but I could not but be
pleased at what he had written.

But such incidents as this were solitary among the
more alarming occasions on which his anger or his
complete loss of recognition of the places and times in
which he found himself created embarrassment and
then danger. This culminated in a display of piety in
Stamford, in the presence of a great number of people.
My father lost all sense of time and place and seemed to
be further away from the day-to-day living we were in
than at any other time.

I sent word of this to Dr Allen at High Beach and he
advised us to watch my father carefully, for he feared this
might lead to something more dangerous. The delusions
continued, with imaginings and rantings and weaknesses,
and in the end, with my father's admission, or half-
admission, that Mary Joyce was dead, it became
impossible that my mother should live a normal life in
such abnormal circumstances. It was settled that he
should be taken to Northampton asylum. He had stayed
with us a good time and now it was apparent that he
could stay no longer.

For a number of days before leaving us he talked of
little else but hellfire and damnation. He seemed
convinced that only these rewards awaited him after his

life was over. At every turn he would talk of the sinfulness of his life and then of the horrible pains that awaited him in eternity. He seemed to have lost all faith in the goodness of himself and in the beauty of the world, a beauty he had so long suckled from and the sense of which he had instilled in all of his children. Nothing could shake him from the terror of death and hell.

He would sit in our kitchen decrying his life and when my mother would say 'God is good', he would shout about his loss of faith in God. Or he would murmur on about the loves of his life and conclude with something such as 'I have loved much but there is none left to love, I have done with it'.

He stayed with us that Christmas of eighteen hundred and forty-one. It was a sombre time, overshadowed by the knowledge that two doctors had certified my father fit only for admission to St Andrew's Hospital for Mental Diseases. My brother and I had had this certification done, for my mother would not and yet she could not carry on. And so we celebrated our Christmas as a family, all of us knowing, except for my father, that he would be leaving us within the week. Two days after Christmas and two days before he left us, my mother told him that he must go back to the asylum for treatment.

'To High Beach?' he asked.

'No,' my mother said, 'to Northampton. It is not such a great way off.'

'No,' he said. 'I shall be close for coming home.'

She nodded to him and he seemed satisfied in that.

The following day I walked with him to the edge of the fen and he asked me to wait while he crossed to the four oaks that grew on the pasture's limit. He had a great fondness for them and he went and spoke quietly and hugged each of them in turn. I think, when he was hugging farewell to the oaks, he was saying farewell to all of us and to all of his life in Helpston and Northborough.

And so he left us on the twenty-ninth day of December of that year, the year's end, for Northampton and the asylum there. The doctor who came to accompany him on his journey told me that he blamed my father's illness on years 'addicted to poetical prosings'. I could not think of any right reply to this.

We stood outside and my mother walked with him from the house to the coach. I could not help but think of the joy of his coming home six months earlier. Just before he climbed into the carriage with the doctor, he turned to me and he spoke.

'Do the primroses still grow in the churchyard?' he asked.

'Yes, Father,' I said. 'In their season.'

He nodded and said 'good', and then climbed inside.

My father was never to see his wife again, or his village.

I would go and visit with him when I could. That was not often but I tried to see him once in every two years. Sometimes he would sit, during my visit, saying nothing and I would sit with him, knowing there was no word I could say to break him out of where he was. If the weather was at all clement he would sit in the garden of the asylum. It was strange to see him among the flowers and trees, seeming so peaceful, when he might have sat among his own flowers in his own garden, with his own people. But each time I thought of enquiring, and the few occasions that I did, I was told it was not possible for him to come back home. Yet. And yet became two years and then four and then a decade. Twenty-three years in all.

But sometimes he would be talkative. His conversation would always be of the past and the freedom it had given him. Once, he talked of nothing but his times in London. Nothing else seemed to exist in his head but those weeks when he had visited the city and had been introduced to the great writers and painters. And yet at the end of it all, his speech became deeper and more quiet.

'I were walking past St Paul's cathedral,' he told me. 'I saw an African, a black man, sitting in the street asking alms. He were more lost than I was. So far from home, like me, but I leastways could go back home. I passed him by and all that night I thought as how I should have given him a shilling. I went back the next day and the next and the next but I never saw him again.'

And those were the last words he spoke to me that day. Always, I came away with a feeling of terrible sadness. And now that he could no longer do my mother direct hurt by going off with other women or stabbing her with his words and the sharpness of his spoken memories, I felt more and more for him. He never waved me goodbye when I left. I seemed to drift out of his mind before I had gone and he seemed as though he was cutting my presence off before I could do it myself.

Sometimes when I visited he would think he was someone else. A wrestler or a bare-fist fighter or even Lord Byron, the poet. And another time he told me as how he saw Lord Byron's funeral and he in London, with empty carriages behind the hearse. 'Ne'er a person in any carriage,' he said. And he told me how he stood and watched it pass.

On the times when he would talk with me I would ask him how his writing went and he would tell me the poems he had written. Even at his worst times he could read and recite his verses to me and it was a joy to hear them flow. He had a gift of memory when it came to verse. It dated back, I believe, to days when he would find verses while he was out walking the fens, without a paper on which to write. He would memorise the words and come back home, perhaps half a day later or even the next day, with the words still clear within his head.

I was not the only visitor to my father's place of detention. There were several in each year but they were people who knew nothing of him as a man and came only because of what they had heard or read. And they were strangers to him. They did nothing to allay his fears or warm his loneliness. He was merely a spectator at their spectating and he knew it.

In most of his days he would sit on the roadside, watching the children at play, observing the passing carts, and scribble in one of his pocketbooks, but at other times he would stand in the garden of the asylum, gazing, as a child would, into the sky, entranced for hours by something inside his head. Imagining what might follow on a better day? The thought has crossed my mind though I have no reason for thinking so.

There were times when I brought bad news to my father. And there were times when it seemed the only news I brought. Two years after he entered Northampton asylum it was I who brought him word of my brother Frederick's death. He was twenty years old and my grief was compounded by having to speak of it to my father. He sent a letter to the family which I carried on my return, urging us 'to behave well to your mother'. A year later I was back in his company to tell him of my sister Anna's death. She was twenty-four years old and her death brought back a torrent of memories, for my mother had been pregnant with Anna when she and my father married. In one afternoon, he relived again the tempestuous days of their marrying, his doubts and his fleeing the village for a time. Those memories seemed to occupy his mind more than Anna's death. It was, I imagine, his way of painting the present over with the colours of the past. Finally, in that twisting trickle of sadness, I travelled in the March of eighteen hundred and forty-six to tell my father of his own father's death.

He sat a long time on hearing the news from me and then he said: 'I had thought him dead this good many years.'

'He lived a good long life,' I said.

'Love cannot be made to grow where no love is,' my father replied and left his comments at that.

My mother, all this time, dealt with the living and the dead in our home. She it was who laid out my brother and my sister and my grandfather in their turns. She it was who looked to their burying. She it was who accepted the sympathies of the village and she it was who despatched me, finding the fare from God knew what place, to tell my father of the news.

My other brothers did what little was to be done in helping. John went about his life and became an inspector of bridges. William worked our land and hired himself to farmers in Northborough and Helpston. Charles took upon himself many of our debts, paid from his clerk's wage, until he too died, in the year of eighteen hundred and fifty-two. I did not bring that news to my father. I could not, for I had not seen him in three years and to arrive with another tale of loss was more than I could bear. Instead I wrote to his doctor and asked that he should tell the news.

Letters would come to us at the oddest intervals, some quite sane, some quite beyond our reckoning, some at peace and some complaining that we had not sent him books he had asked of us. He would give most detailed instructions as to where the volumes might be found upon such and such a shelf, but in the greater part these were volumes he had long ago lost or given to someone.

In telling all of this I know I bring my own memories, as they are, to bear upon the facts but these are the memories which surface first. There are others. I have memories of my father heartily laughing; of his love of laughter; of his clever way with words; of the warmth of his greeting; of the beauty of his verses; of the closeness of his arm about my waist as we went walking through the grounds of Northampton asylum. But these are not the first things I think of. They come only with an effort because they are not how I imagine my father to have been in that dark, misty uncertainty that was his mind for all of my adult life.

Of course I do not know how he truly felt or what the real thought was that kept his other thoughts together. I can only surmise and in doing so I find myself drawn again and again to a darkness in his life. What man, even the heartiest and most open to the ways of nature, could be content with a life that ended so slowly and in such lonely circumstances? When I look from side to side, from my father to my mother, I see them both in isolation, battling against the vagaries of a life that had been cruel in weaving a rope of hope and then using it to tie them separately to illness and poverty and the heartbreak of death upon death in a time when their lives might have been easier.

When I saw him among the other men at Northampton I could not but think, as I knew he did constantly, of his times in London and of the company he had treasured and of the days he spent in the company of people who encouraged him and treated him as his talent deserved. But the kindnesses of his patrons were never without the expectation of some return. They never possessed the unselfish devotion of which my father was capable. Each small generosity had a purpose and, indeed, many took more than will ever be known. They stripped my father of everything – even the respect that gave resolve to his life.

And then my mother, labelled 'the widow Clare', although her husband was hale and hearty in his body, going about her life as though there was a purpose to it, when all the purpose had been ground out of her by her own sickness and the loss of her family.

All of this comes easily to my mind. The brighter days are deep, too deep to find with ease. Too deep.

And yet, at times when I felt most lost, most hopeless in his company, he might utter one sentence and set me thinking. Such a time came at the end of a long day I had spent with my father in the summer of eighteen hundred and fifty-nine. I had sat with him while he finished his evening meal. It was a day of great heat and even at that late hour we went and sat in the garden and watched the sky for all the signs of another warm day to come. We had sat a great time in silence when my father spoke.

'Genesis is a paltry piece of work. Now John's gospel is where the real tale is told,' he said.

I had heard him say that once before, another summer's evening, in the days before he had been sent away in the first place. My mother had sent me to fetch him from the Blue Bell and when I went in he was talking with some men and he was saying that very same thing. And here he was saying it again, so many years later.

'The clergy preach Genesis as if there were no other book,' he said that evening, from the doorway. And then he walked home with me, leaning upon my arm and telling me I was a good girl.

Other evenings he'd return from walking the fens,

with a long scrawl of lines, and while he ate his supper
I'd read them back to him. There was one I was always
most fond of and still am. I think of it when I am
troubled about the life he lived and I think of it, without
an effort, when I remember his happiest times.

> Up this green woodland ride lets softly rove
> And list the nightingale – she dwelleth here.
> Hush let the wood gate softly clap – for fear
> The noise may drive her from her home of love.

I think of that and I see my father, his finger to his lips
to quiet my chattering, listening for the birds of the
wood; I see him gently closing the gate behind us, the
timbered latch deadened by his fingers.

But for every such memory there is another that
comes to undermine it. The times when my father
would slip away to see some woman. All that pretence
of no one knowing when my mother knew right well
and when, in time, those of us old enough to know
knew what was happening. But our mother went on
with her life and ours, knowing my father would return.
But why should she have had to go through that? And
why should we?

I recall one event from the year of Anna's death. That
autumn a young man came calling on me, frequently,
and walked with me and was at my beck and call. He was
in love with me and I with him, I think. And that
Christmas he called to take me dancing to a house dance

in Market Deeping. I was in a state of despair at that time. It had been a year of loss and illness in our family, and he had called every evening in that month to sit with my mother and me and had arranged to have someone sit with my mother while we were away. I was happy to go with him and I had resewn an old white dress of Anna's and made of it a dress of my own for that night. He had brought a trap and we sped the miles to Market Deeping, under a bright quartered moon.

As we were entering the house where the party was being held, he handed me a sheet of paper and bade me read it at my leisure. This I did once the opportunity came. It was a verse he had written for me. I thanked him for it, as we danced, and later, at supper, he told me he had a great deal of verse written.

'I should like to have it published in books,' he said. 'I should like to be a poet such as your father.'

I knew then that he meant what he said; it was not to impress me, it was his intention. And I knew too that he had spoken the epitaph on our love without knowing it. I could not face the thought of another writer in my life, I could no longer trust him despite his kindness. I could never tell him why I had begun at once to grow cold in my affections, for he would not have understood, the reason being inexplicable to any but myself. My mother would have understood in some way but I did not explain to her. Perhaps, of all, my father would most clearly have understood my fears but he was not to know of my predicament. I recall the journey home that night as one might recall a funeral of a loved one or as a soul might recall its own separation and observation of the body left behind. The moon was as bright and the night as sharp as when we had journeyed outward but now there was a terrible coldness within.

Of course, life might have gone sweetly and one man may not be like another, but I had had my fill of poems and poets. I had my father still to think of and in doing so I could not escape the shadow his darkness cast.

But enough of that. To return to my father's life. In his last years he was afflicted with a great many illnesses. His sight was poorly and I was sent for at one time because his delusions had grown more stubborn. He would no longer answer to his own name but only to that of Lord Byron. It was hoped that the sight of my face might bring some recognition of his true self. I stayed in Northampton two days at that time and sat with him a great deal. In private I would ask him if he knew who he was and he would nod.

'You are John Clare, Father,' I would say. 'You are not Lord Byron.'

'Aye,' he would agree, 'but I was Byron. Now I am John Clare.'

But this delusion, too, seemed to dissolve in the months that followed my visit.

At the Christmastide of eighteen hundred and sixty-two I wrote my father a long letter, reminding him of a Christmastide years before when he and I had walked home from market together, me prattling on about all we had seen, and he had stopped in the roadway and held my attention with the straight look of his blue eyes and said one sentence to me: 'Anticipation is the sweetest of earthly pleasures.'

I reminded him of that in writing, for it had occupied my own mind greatly in all that month. He replied in the early days of the following month, calling me his 'dear daughter' and telling me how much he missed me and my mother and recalling the happier days when he had worked with his hands and felt the better and clearer for it.

I have thought a great deal of late about that phrase which came back to me and inspired my letter to him. I think that dedication to anticipation of pleasure made him much the way he was. A man always waiting for Mary Joyce and never being quite fulfilled by anything within his life. In seeing that I have seen, beyond doubt, that none of us failed him in any way. Nothing we could have done within the family could have made his life in any way better or sweeter. Nothing that his closest friends and patrons could have done would truly have softened his life.

The last occasion on which I went to visit him was in

the October of eighteen hundred and sixty-three, a seven month before he died. He had been confined for more than two years to the gardens of the asylum but in the February of that year he had lost the use of his legs and been committed to bed. At the summer's end he seemed to regain his strength and when I visited him I wheeled him in a chair into the garden. I had been warned of his growing coarseness of tongue but I heard nothing of it in my two days with him.

As we sat in the garden on my last afternoon with him he was, for the most of our time, quiet but he talked occasionally. It was not a pleasant conversation but rather one in which his failures seemed to rise like demons about him.

'There were a time when I thought as I should never fail,' he said to me. 'I failed. How could I fail?'

'You did not fail, Father,' I said.

'Writing has ruined me,' he said quietly and then he became agitated in the extreme. 'They have cut the top off my head and taken out all the vowels so I cannot write.' He was shouting by then and I calmed him by easing my fingers through his hair, as you would a child. When he had settled himself once more, I tried to reassure him.

'Oh, Father,' I said, 'you will write again.'

My only thought then was that he should not become disillusioned beyond hope. I had no thought of the hardness he had brought into our lives but only of the softness I might instil in his old mind.

'I have lost the language,' he said. 'I spoke it once and one other spoke it but I cannot speak it alone.'

And with that he seemed to have withdrawn again into himself but suddenly, and with a great degree of strength in his voice and with a light in his eyes, he went on speaking, urgently, looking straight into my eyes as he did.

'The last time I saw her it were a russet evening this time of year and the apples hung in bunches from the trees.'

And then his eyes seemed to cloud and he squinted and looked about him and searched the sky for something before returning his gaze, questioningly, to me.

'Or were there flowers on the whitethorn?' he asked.

I made no answer and immediately he went on.

'We were two children, yet when I touched her hand my heart would turn chill for fear of rejection. But oftentimes I fancied I saw her brush a tear from her face. Her heart were as tender as a bird's, yet she grew to think her station above mine. Her parents were farmers and had pretensions, something my passion could not match.'

His voice faded as he spoke. In a way I was pleased with what I had heard for it brought, at last but not too late, a recognition that Mary Joyce had not been the warm creature he had imagined in his earlier years. That much had been recognised.

I was lost in such thoughts when he spoke again.

'Take me inside,' he whispered. 'I am tired. I should like to sleep now.'

I had some feeling, some premonition, as I prepared to leave the asylum that evening that I might not see my father again. I went back to watch him sleep and thought he was still awake and spoke to him.

'Did you ever write to her or speak to her, to Mary Joyce, in her last years, Father?'

His breathing was soft and settled and he made no answer. I left with uncertain emotions. I knew he was ill in the extreme but I could not but be pleased that this other delusion had at last been laid to rest with her corpse.

The month of May of eighteen hundred and sixty-four was a dry, hot month before its time. On the tenth day of that month my father had another seizure and we were notified. But none of us could go to be with him. He died in the late afternoon of the twentieth day of May, a Friday. They sent word to us on the next day. My mother was poorly herself at that time but she set about preparing for my father's return.

He had passed away on a day when the hedges were alive with the confetti of the whitethorn and the primroses and cowslips were heavy in the dykes. It was as hot as a day in June.

My father's coffin arrived before our preparations were complete and it lay in the Blue Bell before his burying. We followed it to the churchyard and saw him safe at last in the earth he had walked, and written and spoken and sung of, all his life. There was a final comfort in that but it was a sadness to me that none of us was there to see him off on his last journey into death.

I was left on that day, the day of his burying, with sorrow and with satisfaction. Sorrow on his lost life, satisfaction on his return among us. But I was left with a great tiredness too. All of my life had been a part of his. I seemed to feel the need to be his support from when first I learned to walk. This, perhaps, is something my brothers and sisters felt in turn. I never spoke of it with them, but until the day of my father's death I seemed constantly to search for an answer to so many of the griefs his life created in mine. And then when he was dead I felt only regret and satisfaction but not serenity.

And now that feeling of tiredness persists so that I do not want to talk or think again of the vicissitudes of our lives with my father. I need never talk of him again. I have told you all that I can recall. But to dismiss him from my thoughts would be as unnatural as it would be impossible. I can only hope that the pictures which appear uninvited are as pleasant as those I choose to recall.

V

John Clare

M Y DEAREST LOVE,

this is the fifth day of the Maytime and of my seventy-first summer to the world. These last nights of spring, like many of the nights of this winter and of all the winters since childhood, I have lay here in my bed and felt the form of your body next to mine and held it in my arms. But there be nights when I long for more, for kissing you in the places of secrecy, for the shape of your body and the touch of your hand. I long for the particular scent which

I may drink in as apple scent in the autumn. I long, too, for the rarer, deeper scent.

Do you recall a day and us walking together, you and me and Richard Turnill, tramping the road from your home to Helpston? I recall it more and more now. A day deep in the folds of winter and us on the road without a thought for the weathers about us and you bright as sunshine despite the day. We walked in that snowy day, the snow come down on us and we cared nothing for it, trudging on, no doubt, though our feet seemed hardly to notice the miles and we were so lost we never noticed my sister in wait for us beneath a tree, sheltering from the snow. Us three walking. What I would give for us to be back there walking again, wind or snow, I would care not. Walking. Thought of that often concerns me. I thought of it and I walking from High Beach to you or to the hope of you. I felt you there with me as I feel your presence these many nights but when I turned for your comfort there was nothing.

But still there are other memories I have that come to me and you are not seen in them but you are there. Most at this time of the year I remember the great tossing shoulders of whitethorn in the hedges of Helpston, though they were not so great at Northborough. At Glinton they were white as sheets for you and you passed among them with the blueness of bird eggs that were your eyes and the ease of a girl who is free of sin.

As you were and are, unlike John Clare.

Was it not Maytime, too, when we last spoke together face to face without the need for darkness or spirit between us? At Langley Bush before it was destroyed. The whitethorn was a wedding dress about you though I did not say as much for fear of hurting you, even as you were intent on hurting me and bidding farewell with all our lives still before us, and for what? To satisfy the family circumstance and your father's expectations? I would have dropped all expectations tied to a stone into Round Oak Waters if I had thought you might have been for me and without a hesitation, without as much as a glance at where they sank and how and yet you talked of circumstance as if that should satisfy my mind. It never did. And nor yours, I think.

I had much to say to you then and much that was said but no answer to you when you said I must find someone else who would support me in what I had laid out for myself, for you could not and would not. You spoke it as though my need was something new and unknown to you when all the time till then my need was matched only by the need of one other and that was you. To throw my need in my face was a great cut to me among all the cuts we each inflicted that evening. That most beautiful of evenings. A time we had often been together and I had always looked to, that time between work and sleep, a time when dreams are sowed. Now and since I think of evenings as a time when others are left wandering without a home and must look in on the windows in passing and never share the comfort and companionship within. And if I needed what you could not give, have I not in the time since then been careful not to burden you with my need? In the nights when my need has been greatest my loss has been greatest and I have only your memory to mesmerise and harry me. To think of you sleeping in that distant bed is no consolation and no source of joy but only of pain. When I close my arms with longing, the longing is increased. I have talked to you, slept with you, dreamed of you, walked with you, kissed you, touched you and imagined your touch in my own but I have not gone back on what in the end you demanded of me. Instead I set myself to quietness again. When the storm of your absence and my longing blows harshly against itself I set myself to quiet whisperings of your name, your tender name, to the slightest touch of my lips against your phantom skin.

I am no longer afeared of spectres as I was in my childhood, wishing only that yours would come even for a moment to my side, that I might touch and taste you. We have lay in darkness and I thought no word could bring us closer and no word could keep us apart. I looked to death as a welcome state, as a place and time where you already were and where we could be without the circumstances that kept us so long apart in this mad

. world. And then, of late, I dreamed that I woke in paradise and you were there as you promised and I spoke with you, I spoke the warmest whisperings of love and passion and you looked at me with your soft blue eyes, as you were used to, and asked my name and did not remember me at all. And I awoke in tears and called to you, my beloved, in the terror of the grey morning and none came but another prisoner in this madhouse and he stroked my head and stared at me and stroked my head again, most gently, and then went away. None came but him.

And I still call to you, my love, and am calling to you still. I recall you as a girl singing that song you did so sweetly, swinging about the deathstones and singing to me.

Will you go to the rolling of the stones, the tossing of
  the ball,
or will you go and see pretty Susie dance among them
  all,
will you drink of the blood, the white wine and the red
or will you go and see pretty Susie when that I am
  dead?
Susie charmed the birds from the sky, the fish from out
  the waves
and there she'd lie in her true love's arms and there was
  content to stay.

I have never lain with Susie or no one since seeing you. Lie with me now.